"Don't be," he whispered, his breath hot and heavy as he breathed his words against my skin, allowing his breath to caress me. His hands gripped me tightly through my clothing and I was slightly surprised by his actions. Kisten always maintained an incredibly careful and calm demeanor, always distancing himself from me when he thought he was losing control. He growled softly, his voice sounding animalistic. "You're all that I want now."

CATCH A RAVEN
SEALED BLOOD
BOOK ONE

KIRRO BURROWS

To Maria Croft
Who never gave up on me.

To Sara Gardiner,
For helping me get here.

To my beautiful daughter,
Who taught me to do what makes me happy.

PROLOGUE

'*You need to go now.*'

"I know," I whispered back quietly, gently leaning on the door as I checked the hallway. No guards, no sign of any of the First. If I was going to make my escape, I knew I had to do it now. I grabbed the wooden trinket as it hung against my exposed bosom, taking a deep breath as I prepared myself for what I was about to do. There would be no turning back once I left the room, no chance to return.

'*Now!*' As my sister's voice ran through my mind, I darted into darkness, quickly making my way down the Hallway. I ran straight to the crossing I had been escorted by so many times, doing my best to remember the directions my sister had given me. *Left, Left, Straight, Right, Right, no wait, Left.* I did my best to move as silently as I could, barely daring to breathe as I ran. The castle felt still, silent, as if everyone within was sleeping as Mother slept.

It wasn't often that Mater Vitae slept: she only tended to sleep after expending great amounts of power, and I wasn't sure what she had done to warrant this surprise slumber. All I knew was that it was probably my last chance to flee and if I didn't take it now, I would never get another. Mother knew my secret and it was only a matter of time before she decided I was too dangerous to exist, just as she had done to Them.

"Who goes?!" My heart pounded to life as I heard a voice, and I quickly pressed myself into the shadows of the stone, thankful for my dark skin as I melted into the darkness. I watched slowly as a light approached the crossing, and one of the guards came into view. Their stern face wore an annoyed expression and it was obvious they didn't want to be wandering the corridors of the castle at night. "Who dares slink about while Mother sleeps?"

I did my best to silence my breathing, gripping the wooden cross tightly as it grew warm beneath my hand. *So close;* we were so close to freedom. I could *feel* the fresh air pouring in from the door to my right, fresh air I had not breathed in centuries. Mother rarely let me out of my room and let me outside even less. She always knew that I would run if she did not keep a tight hold on my chain, but now it was fear that forced me to attempt my escape.

"Why cause such a noise at this hour?" I couldn't help the relief that filled me as I heard one of the First approach the guard, drawing the man's attention. I could feel the vampire's aura as they drew closer to me, and I could only hope they would not sense me in the same way. I saw her shadow as she stopped near him, and I couldn't help my slight feeling of sympathy as I heard him stumble over his words.

"M-m-my apologies, I-I thought I heard some—"

"No one would dare disturb Mother's rest so callously," the vampire interrupted, her voice stern and almost melodic as she spoke. I watched as her shadow passed that of the guard, and I saw her piercing blue eyes as she stepped into my view. She glanced around the hallways, and I could have sworn her eyes rested on me for a moment, but her gaze continued as she spoke. "As suspected, none are about. You would do best to keep your voice down, lest Mother take her anger out on you next."

"Y-y-y-yes, Nisaba." The man bowed, taking his light with him as he walked back down the corridor. The First seemed to linger in the growing darkness, her long white hair moving in an unknown wind as she shook her head. When she spoke next, my heart stopped beating.

"Be quick, she will awaken soon." She kept her back to me as she spoke, following after the guard as she whispered her quiet words. I was frozen to the spot, surprised by what I had witnessed. Had... one of the First... just helped me?

'You heard her, let's go! We have to leave before Mater Vitae wakes up.' My sister's voice once again roused me from my stupor, and I released the cross as it grew warm under my hand. A moment later I slipped out the door into the quiet night air, not bothering to close it behind me. I took a moment just to breathe in the fresh night air, my lungs swelling with the sweet sensation. I could feel my sister's annoyance with my pause, but the soft taste of freedom was exhilarating. Releasing the breath, I opened my eyes, staring at the garden before me.

I carefully made my way across the courtyard, praying to the Gods I could outrun the Hunter Mother would send after me. My thoughts returned to the vampire and a soft sound escaped me as I pushed aside a low-hanging branch. She *had* to know Vitae would find out, and Mother's wrath would know no end once she did. Not only had Nisaba known I was there, she purposefully allowed me to escape: there was no gain in it for her, was there? Maybe she planned to pin the blame on the naive guard?

'Stop wondering why and just be happy she did. Who knows why vampires do anything they do.' My sister snapped and I sighed as I carefully climbed the wall, looking down on the forest below. She was right as always, and I had a long night ahead of me if I wanted to see the dawn. As I dropped from the stone and sprinted through the trees, I couldn't help the quiet words as they escaped me.

"Thank you, Nisaba."

I

"Well, enjoy your weekend!"

"Huh? Oh, 'bye." I waved to my co-workers as I slammed the hood of my trunk, pulling myself from the fog my thoughts had slipped into. I slid into my green Lexus and pulled away from the airport, my hands gripping the wheel tightly. It would be a long drive back home, and a thoughtful one; I had arrived back from Neo-Kansa after investigating another murder in my current case and while I enjoyed the chance to travel the country freely, I enjoyed living in The Capital and being home more.

Besides, my current case was anything but enjoyable: always arriving too late to prevent the crime was frustrating for the whole team, but especially for me. Any crime can be horrifying and difficult to accept, but this was especially true of crimes committed by Supernaturals, since our abilities allowed us to be far more deadly. By the time my team was called in, the case was a mess and that was never a good situation to be in.

And this case was the definition of a bad situation. Bodies piled up in rooms with no signs of entry, and the perpetrator was able to bypass magical barriers. The list of Supernaturals that could do that was small, and every theory seemed to be killed by the next crime. We had no luck in narrowing it down to even that aspect of who our killer was, and I was beginning to get more and more frustrated with the case.

Before I could dwell on it further, my phone began to ring, the sound distracting me from my spiraling thoughts. I knew who it was before I even began to dig around for my earpiece, sighing heavily as I did so. It was only so long until my boss discovered the plans his daughter and I had made for his Sunday, and I doubted he was happy about it.

"What, Brandon?" I answered, not attempting to hide my annoyance. He scowled on the other end, clearly sharing my sentiment. I could hear he was also driving home, although I knew he lived closer to the airport than I did.

"When was I going to learn about this meeting you set up between me and that... that thing?"

"First of all, Arkrian is not a thing: he's your daughter's fiancé and *Shannon* is the one who set everything up. I merely told her when you would be free." I sighed again, knowing this would be an unpleasant conversation. "There are far worse things to be in this world than a shapeshifter, Brandon."

"How dare you say that, after what that *animal* did to my—"

"Stop right there! That has *nothing* to do with Shannon and Arkrian." I hated having the same argument repeatedly, and I'm sure Shannon was too, which is why she asked for my help. "We *both* know

6

that. Your hatred for what Kynagi did is justified, no one is arguing that. But you cannot keep blaming all shifters for what one did."

"I don't want him anywhere near my daughter, much less me. Why Shannon insists on this bullshi–"

"I wasn't finished yet, *Boss*." I growled through gritted teeth to keep certain words from spilling out as I adjusted my grip on the wheel. The fact that he was being unfair and extremely judgmental of Arkrian didn't matter, there are certain things you don't say to your boss. "Secondly, I know Arkrian personally, and he wouldn't do anything he knows you don't approve of. For crying out loud, you haven't even met him! That's why Shannon set up that damn dinner for you guys: so you could try to get to know him because, whether you like him or not, Shannon *will* marry him."

Silence on the other end. Brandon might not have liked it, but he knew I was right. Shannon had strongly voiced that if her father refused to give her away, she would have her brother do it, who was already a part of the Supernatural community thanks to his vampire bride. It was largely Mark's secret marriage to a vampire that had Brandon so upset about Shannon also marrying a Supernatural, and a shifter at that. Although he swore that it wouldn't affect his judgment on the job, it was obvious that he still blamed all shifters and Supernaturals in general for his wife's loss. It must've seemed like a betrayal for both of his children to fall in love with non-humans, but that didn't justify his behavior.

"I'm hanging up on you now, Brandon. All Shannon and I ask is that you give him half a chance, because if you don't, you're going to lose both of your children. I'd rather not see that happen." I hung up as I pulled into the driveway of my home, parking in my garage as the door opened automatically. I dragged myself out of the car, hoping to relax on my couch as I slammed the door, not bothering to retrieve my luggage from the trunk.

My hopes were instantly dashed as I stepped into my home, however, as a tugging began in the back of my mind. The Overseer was calling me toward him, but I did my best to ignore the command as I stepped into the kitchen. Lucius *had* to know I had just gotten back from my case, and the last thing I felt like doing was playing babysitter to the Coven.

Searching my fridge for anything to settle my thoughts and dumping out old food, I decided on a bottle of yogurt, not wanting to put in the effort to cook. Slamming the fridge with my foot and ignoring the bill from the pet sitter, I made my way back to my living room, where Lira and Xris sat waiting for me. I knew I didn't have time for them but couldn't resist the desire to rest for a few moments while I did my best to ignore the Overseer. My two pretties jumped into my lap as soon as I plopped on my couch, both begging for my undivided attention. Petting with one hand and eating with the other, I gave them both attention as best I could, but my mind was elsewhere and the constant tugging wasn't helping, either. Soon, both cats were meowing their disappointment in my performance.

"Well, you didn't have me for long anyway. Lucius is being a dick, and I have to go pick up someone." I scoffed, pushing them both out of my lap as I stood. I wearily walked down the hall to my bedroom, groaning as I pushed the door open. Tossing my clothing on an ever-growing pile of dirty clothes, I searched through my closet, changing into a simple blue shirt and shorts. My cats followed my every move, tangling themselves in my steps as they begged me to stay with their purrs and meows.

Forcing myself outside and climbing wearily back into the car, I pulled away from my empty shell of a home and began cruising back toward Decver. Out of all the cities in The Capital, it was by far the biggest that remained, but more importantly for me, it was the safest. Vitae's Hunters were always searching for me, and it was only by moving whenever they got close that I had managed to avoid them for as long as I had. In a Governance as large as The Capital, I would have plenty of notice before a Hunter could reach me in Decver.

The sound of my phone ringing forced me out of my thoughts, and I huffed once I saw the name. I generally made it a rule not to talk while driving, but I had to make an exception for Lucius' Coven and my boss. Although I had only taken on the role reluctantly, part of my job in the Coven was to be available to Lucius' people in case he couldn't be, which unfortunately included other Coven members.

"Raiven speaking." I tapped my earpiece as I switched lanes, once again not trying to hide my annoyance.

"Hurry, Raiven, it's already past eight." It was Crispin, First in the Coven and a vampire I absolutely could not stand. He had texted me as soon as I landed to come pick him up from his outing, since apparently Lucius wanted him for something. I had absolutely no intention of picking him up, but now that I was also on my way to Lucius, I lacked a good excuse not to. "Where are you?"

"On the bridge." I felt the familiar bump as I got on the bridge, switching lanes to pass the slow driver in front of me. "It does take a while to get there from my house."

"Your house? I thought you were at the airport."

"No." I retorted. "I went home first."

"Thought gas was too expensive for you to waste." He teased, and I groaned as I did my best not to respond to the obvious bait. Technically, my whole make of car was illegal: gas engines had long been replaced with electric cars and being caught driving a guzzler would result in large fines and an impounded car. However, this car had seen me to hell and back: I would not give her up so easily.

"I hadn't planned on wasting it," I finally answered, glancing at the time as I noticed my exit. "I'll be there soon."

"Just hurry." Turning off onto the state road, I began to move my stuff from the passenger seat as I sat at the light. I wasn't used to having other people in my car, so any seat that I wasn't in was fair game for papers, my gun, and a plethora of trash. I did my best to shove it all onto the backseat, pulling into the parking lot where I saw Crispin waiting. Despite the fact the sun had set hours ago, Crispin's golden hair still seemed to glow as he walked up to me.

"Thanks Rai." He collapsed against the seat as I pulled back into traffic. "I owe you."

"Forget it." I brushed him off as I headed toward our Overseer, annoyed by the ever-growing traffic and the tugging in my mind. I knew it was a holiday weekend, and many were eager to head downtown, but it annoyed me all the same. "Lucius was calling me anyway. Otherwise, I'd be home right now."

"Good. I just hope that Eve isn't there." He sighed, closing his eyes as he slumped further in the seat. His simple shirt was unbuttoned at the top and his dark jeans hugged him tightly, but I tried not to notice as I glanced at him. Crispin was being unusually polite for once and besides that, he never shortened my name for any reason. My eyes continued drifting over him and I noticed something shiny around his wrist.

"That new?" I nodded to the watch, and then grew worried when he didn't answer. Afraid to take my eyes off the road, I reached over to touch it, activating my power slightly. The moment my fingers brushed it, I knew it contained silver and couldn't help my slight scowl. I yanked it off, tossing it out the window and angrily gripping my wheel as it bounced in the road. "For fuck's sake, Mikael, maybe next time ask about the composition before you buy stupid jewelry.

"Sorry, I meant Crispin." I quickly corrected myself, cursing internally as I realized my mistake. I felt it as his power reacted to me using his human name and I could tell he was staring at me even as I avoided meeting his gaze.

"No, what did you call me?" Crispin's voice was suspicious, and he leaned over to touch my arm. I flinched ever so slightly at the touch, but with him so close, there was no way he missed it. His return to normal was unfortunately quick, and I was starting to wish I had left the watch on him. "Did you... just call me Mikael?"

"Sorry," I muttered as we neared The Landing, grateful to be out of the seemingly endless traffic. I kept my eyes on the road and tried to pretend Crispin wasn't there, even as his gaze burned into me. "Sometimes I slip up with the name changes. I'll try not to dead name you again."

"Unlike Lucius, I don't tend to share my human name. How do *you* know that name?" As soon as I parked, he tried to pull me closer, but I pulled away, fighting the urge to slap him. He was right: under normal circumstances, I shouldn't have known his dead name. However, the situation between me and Crispin wasn't normal, and only I knew the reason why. Before I could say anything more, Kisten came into view, saving me from the vampire's interrogation.

"There's Kisten. Let's go before he gets the wrong idea." I quickly climbed out of my car, thankful for his perfect timing. Crispin was about to make it evident that he wasn't done with me when Kisten stopped, staring at us. Kisten's expression was blank as he looked at us, and he seemed a little distracted.

"Does Lucius know you were out, Cris?"

"No," we answered simultaneously, then Crispin continued: "I went out on my own for a bit. Asked for a ride once Lucius called me back."

"Oh," he shrugged, his eyes lingering on me for only a moment before he looked away. A soft look flashed through his chartreuse eyes, but it passed just as quickly as it had appeared. "Well, Evalyn and Lucius are looking for both of you, so I'd hurry. Especially you, Cris."

"Where are you going?" I asked as he continued down the sidewalk, evidently in a hurry to leave. I was surprised when he actually stopped to answer, glancing over his shoulder. His eyes softened again as they met mine and then returned to their sad and gloomy stare.

"Home." He shifted as he took off down the walk, rushing to get away. I watched him disappear into the darkness of the night and turned to catch Crispin walking the way Kisten had come. Silently, I followed in his shadow and chastised myself for my earlier slip-up. Usually, I avoided Crispin like the plague, not only to avoid what had happened earlier, but because I just couldn't stand who he had become.

"Raiven!" Somewhere in my thoughts, I heard Eve's voice and I realized we had reached the back of The Dream. Lucius owned The Landing and many nightclubs in Decver, but The Dream was one of two clubs that allowed humans and Supernaturals to mingle. By default, that also made it one of the more popular night clubs, and considering it was a holiday weekend, tonight seemed to be no exception.

"Raiven, where have you and Crispin been?" She was in her security outfit and, judging by her attitude, was not happy about playing babysitter at the club. Lucius required all his Coven to help with the businesses, and Eve was no exception, as much as she liked to be. Besides that, we were technically coworkers outside of the Coven, and she never got over the fact I was on the Central team while she was stuck on the local. She failed to understand that I had been working with Division 11 since its inception, and merely saw me as a rival in her quest for power.

The ala was glaring at me as if she wanted to eat me alive and I decided I couldn't pass up the chance to make her even more upset. Besides, Crispin had already managed to find his way on my bad side and I was upset that Lucius had even called me here. I grinned as I crossed my arms, ignoring the concerned look on Crispin's face.

"Well, he needed a ride back," I started, and Crispin sighed, relieved that I was telling the truth. I couldn't help my smirk as I continued. "So, I picked him up and brought him here. Then we got freaky in the car and it was *great*. As you can imagine, we didn't want to rush things."

Crispin and Eve glared at me as I smiled and shrugged, but Crispin cut her off before she could say a word. "Leave it, Eve; it's not true. I did need a ride back, but I accidentally called Raiven instead of you. If you don't want me calling her, get your number changed."

At least my lie was fun. I thought, turning away. I guess it helped to cool her down, because she turned from us, her fists curling and uncurling as she sought to control her anger. Eve's cell number was terribly similar to mine, with only the last two numbers being different and she had been encouraged to change her number several times. However, as usual, she saw it as losing to me and refused to concede.

"*Anyway*, both of you need to hurry. Lucius is looking for you." She stomped off into the club, her red hair waving as she left us in the dark parking lot. Crispin and I walked down further, entering a door that would take us beneath The Landing and into the Coven. Climbing down the dimly lit stairs into the earth, Crispin suddenly stopped, and I unerringly ran into him. He whipped around like lightning and pinned me to the wall with his body. Being so close, I knew he felt my heartbeat quicken and I did my best to hide my anger.

"Why is it every time I touch you, your heartbeat

14

quickens? Do I scare you or..." He leaned in close, his breath dancing across my skin. I had to fight the involuntary shudder it caused and instead, I glared at him. He chuckled at my glare, clearly entertained. "Is it more?"

"Because I want your body. Now put me down," I quipped, and Crispin chuckled again, moving as if to bite me. Instead, he lightly kissed my collarbone, and it only enraged me more. I moved my leg as if to kick him, but he quickly shifted his weight to stop me. His eyes swirled with power when he looked up at me, and I knew he was using his inhuman strength to keep me pinned.

"Stop with the bullshit, Raiven. You've turned me down every time I've offered it to you." Crispin's expression turned serious, and I couldn't help the slight fear that crept into me. If it came down to a fight, I could likely win, but Lucius would be furious with both of us fighting in the Coven. "How do you know my human name?"

"Let me down and maybe I'll consider being honest." I stared into his eyes as he let me down, his blue eyes burning with mischief. I didn't appreciate the whole 'pinning me to the wall' part, or the light teasing he had decided to indulge in. I rolled my shoulders a bit and cracked my neck, knowing I was only annoying him. "I'll tell you later, if I feel like it."

"In my room, then," he agreed and continued down the stairs, leaving me enraged on the steps. I felt less like telling him the truth and more like helping him to stake himself. I knew it wouldn't kill him, but it would at least get him out of my hair for the rest of the night.

"Coming?" I snapped from my thoughts and

jogged down the stairs to meet him as he called back to me. We walked down the hallway together, our steps echoing as I matched his stride. I considered smacking him for being an arrogant prick but lost the chance when we reached the living room of the underground space, Crispin opening the heavy doors.

As soon as we stepped into the room, I knew something was off. Lucius usually kept the living room fairly well furnished: a couple of couches, a few armchairs, two TVs on each side and a coffee station so we could gather and talk. However, now most of the furniture had been taken out: only two couches and the coffee spot remained, making the space seem bigger than it ever had appeared before.

"Crispin, Raiven, please sit." Lucius motioned for us to sit on the couch across from him and his guest as soon as he noticed us. Lounging beside him was a caramel-skinned vampire who was all smiles and his eyes followed us as we moved through the room. Justina stood against the far wall next to the coffee, staring off into the distance. I couldn't see her face, but the air in the room was almost suffocating, which meant she was upset about something. Lucius seemed to be ignoring her and continued as we sat, perching on opposite ends of the couch. "I'd like to introduce our guest, LeAlexende, Overseer of the Southern Grove. He will be visiting with us for the Fest of Peace this weekend."

"Welcome to our territory. We look forward to your graces as we bless you with ours." Ignoring the angry sorcerer, I addressed our guest and he nodded, his already wide grin growing wider, emphasizing the oddity of his purple eyes. He tossed his blonde hair as he laughed, clearly pleased with my words.

"The pleasure is indeed mine." LeAlexende's eyes flashed with mirth as he turned to Lucius. "Rare to find someone who knows the traditional greeting. An interesting one indeed, just as you said."

"Yes, indeed," The Overseer agreed, giving LeAlexende a soft smile before addressing us. I glared at him in return, and he shrugged, still smiling. Sometimes Lucius' arrogance to brag about me was as annoying as Crispin thinking he owned every woman in the world. It was no wonder they got along so well. "While Alexende is in our territory, I will allow excursions, but all members of the Coven must remain here, save those who are out of Decver."

I groaned internally at the order but was careful not to show my disappointment on my face as I spoke. "For how long?"

"Until Monday." Three days stuck at the Coven, except for Kisten. According to Eve, he caused too much commotion when he had to stay and was a 'disturbance'. Considering no one had ever seen it and the fact that Kisten was the most mild-mannered person I had ever met, I think she made it up as an excuse to not have him around to influence Lucius. Kisten never wanted to be around anyway, so I guess it was a decision that worked for both of them.

"I'll be here. I have Monday off from the office." I shrugged, doing my best to hide my annoyance. I wasn't close to most of the Coven, and it was always awkward when I was forced to spend time with everyone else. "But I'm on call for an important case, so if it comes, I'm gone."

"You may leave."

I wasn't sure which way he meant it, but I took it for both: I stood up to escape the room. As I walked

17

by, Crispin grabbed my arm, forcing me to pause in my movement. At that moment, Justina glanced up with her green eyes, her deep blue hair rippling. My own power surged through me, and I knew my eyes had grown brighter.

"Strike two, Crispin. Try me for three." I growled, narrowing my eyes at the vampire. I knew it was rude to fight in front of a guest, but Crispin had been working on my nerves ever since I picked him up, making my already bad mood worse. Lucius didn't say a word but the charge in the surrounding air increased, making the already dense air even harder to breathe in. Crispin glanced at Lucius, who maintained his soft smile and polite expression. He slowly released the grip on my arm and turned away from me.

"Crispin, I'd like to speak with you." Lucius' words were still polite as he looked at LeAlexende and Justina. Justina left without so much as a word and LeAlexende nodded as he stood.

"I can take a hint. We can finish catching up later," the tan Overseer walked up to me, opening the door that led to the rest of the Coven. "After you."

"*Gratias*[1]." I passed him and carefully held the door open as he walked through, making sure to close it behind us. It was about time someone talked to Crispin about his manners, or lack thereof.

"By the way, you have an interesting accent, one I have not heard in a long time. I look forward to getting to know you better... Raiven." He flashed another bright smile before walking away, disappearing in the darkness. Steamed by Crispin's actions and Lucius' bragging, I continued to Crispin's room and slammed the door as I entered. On the other side, I heard someone mutter about me being inconsiderate, but I didn't care in the least. I leaned against the door, the weight of my evening trying to drown me. I hated days like this, when it seemed like the Gods were determined to make me as miserable as possible.

Sighing heavily, I forced myself up from the heavy wood and collapsed into his armchair, closing my eyes as I waited.

2

"**R**aiven, is that you?" I opened my eyes as Crispin's door opened, and Justina walked in. A glance at the clock told me I had only fallen asleep for a short while and I rubbed my eyes as she closed the door. If it had been anyone else, I would've helped them see their way out. However, Justina was higher ranked than me and on top of that, I liked her. "Why are you in Cris' room?"

"He wanted to talk in his room." I sighed, relaxing back into his armchair, still annoyed and upset from earlier. Justina sat on the bed across from me, her expression showing how much she didn't believe me. I shrugged, sinking lower into the chair. "I'm finally going to tell him the truth so he'll leave me the hell alone."

"Which one?" she joked lightly, until she registered the annoyed look in my eye. Her face turned serious, and her voice dropped in volume. "Oh, that one... Are you sure you're ready? That he's ready?"

"Should've done it forever ago. I'm so tired of him and besides... I need to do this for myself," I closed my eyes, unable to help the weight that started to settle on my chest. The sorcerer said nothing, waiting patiently for me to continue. "He'll be fine. He's turned into such a womanizer that I doubt it'll bother him that much. I'm the one who's been carrying this."

"You've carried your guilt long enough. Time for you to let go," Justina assured me, studying me. Then: "I'll never stop being amazed by you. It's not common to see someone with dark skin and bright green eyes and your hair is so beautiful and unique. It's a shame you cut it so short."

"Oh, don't you start it too: everyone has been complaining about that. We both know I was sick of all that hair and besides, your eyes are brighter than mine. My eyes are far more hazel most of the time." I pointed out, rubbing my hand over my short afro and Justina laughed, the sound filling the room. I couldn't help my slight smile at the sound, standing from the chair as she stood. I allowed her to take my hands in her own, looking up to meet her gaze as her laughter faded.

"*Ой бай*[1]. I'm Russian, Rai. Green eyes are a part of who I am," I closed my eyes as she kissed my forehead before kissing me gingerly on the lips. I enjoyed kissing Justina, but for her, it was a gesture of closeness and trust. I had learned long ago to accept them as merely that and to quell any thoughts of it being more. "But you are not and that makes you unique. I know you don't like being stuck here with the rest of us, but if you can swallow that pride, you can stay in my room tonight."

"We'll see," I answered softly, reluctantly letting her hand slip from mine, and I fell back into Crispin's chair as she left. I closed my eyes again as she gently closed the door, my thoughts turning to the years I had with Crispin before he was turned. Then, way back then, he was kind, sweet, and thoughtful, just like...

"Raiven." I barely moved as he walked in and closed the door silently behind him. I ran my hand over my hair again, keeping my gaze on Crispin as he sat on his bed, studying him, reading him. Hating what being turned had done to him as I fought not to glare at the vampire. It wasn't his fault, but despite what people love to say, being turned *does* change a person.

"What did Lucius want?" I asked softly.

Crispin scoffed in response as he leaned back on his bed.

"To 'remind' me that I'm not supposed to make a scene in front of guests," he repeated sarcastically, making air quotes as he spoke. "Honestly, I think you made more of a scene than me."

"You started it and you damn well know it." I could feel the anger boiling in my chest again, but I forced myself to swallow it down. "Do you want to know why I know your name, or not?"

"Well, I'm going to guess someone told you." He looked at me coyly, crossing his legs as he leaned back on his bed. Crispin was still handsome, his golden hair always somehow falling exactly right around his shoulders. I found myself tracing the stark line of his collarbone with my eyes, following the line that ran down the center of his chest. His top buttons were still open, showing the muscle he had never had before being turned. His dark pants did little to hide his physique but despite the changes, I couldn't help but trace with my eyes what I had once touched with my hands.

Crispin cleared his throat to get my attention, causing me to jump slightly and raise my eyes to his. His face held a devilish grin, and he lifted his hand to his chest, enticingly tracing the exposed skin there. He knew I had been staring at him and I snorted, turning away from his display.

"Yeah, someone did. *You*," I said plainly, and Crispin laughed, throwing his head back for gravitas. I waited until he decided to stop being dramatic and to see that I wasn't kidding. He let out a loud breath, leaning forward on his elbows as he spoke.

"One would think I'd remember if I did," Crispin scoffed, his blue eyes looking into mine deeply as he tried to read me. I met his gaze evenly, wishing I could run away to Justina's room already as he continued. "Like I said, a precious few have been trusted with that information and I *don't* recall telling *you*."

"That's because it was before you turned." I closed my eyes, sighing heavily as I tried to decide how honest I wanted to be. "You and I were once close friends, maybe more than that. We had met at a party and I guess we hit it off well. I know your memories of before are spotty at best, but..."

"I can't say my recollection is the best, but I think I'd remember you. You are quite unusual after all, and an exquisite beauty, even now." Crispin smiled, his fangs appearing as he gazed at me. He undressed me with his eyes as I had done him, and I didn't appreciate the look. "You are much, much older than me, so you would've already changed by the time you met me."

"I was, and the memories might start to surface someday, if I stay here." I sighed internally as I mused. "We spent a lot of time together back then, in the comfort of each other's embrace. But..."

"Oh?" The dark hint that entered his expression as he interrupted me was enough to make me stand and move for the door. However, he was faster and managed to pin me to it, preventing me from leaving. Crispin pressed himself into me, placing his hand over mine on the handle as he kept me pinned to his door. He slid his free hand down my back, gingerly lifting the edge of my top and tracing the skin above my shorts, teasingly playing with the small of my back. I had to fight the desire to arch my back towards him and tried to ignore his playful touch as he whispered into my ear, his voice deep and sultry.

"Well, maybe you should use your embrace to remind me. Perhaps I might remember if I had a taste," I closed my eyes, focusing on my anger before whipping around sharply. He must not have expected me to react so violently, because he was easily tossed back by my movement. His eyes showed shock for a moment, before returning to their devilish intent. "It's an honest suggestion, Raiven."

"Back then, my embrace meant something to you. *I* meant something to you," I spat, taken aback by my tone as I spoke. I was angry, but I was also... hurt. Hurt in a way I thought I had long overcome. "Enough that you wanted–"

I stopped myself, covering my face as I kept the words from spilling out. I owed Crispin the truth, I knew that, but I hadn't expected how much I still cared about him. How much I still hated myself for being the reason he was turned. I took a deep breath before dropping my hands, unable to help the anger in my eyes as I looked at him again.

"But now that you've turned, you're no longer that person. You're selfish, arrogant and nothing like the person I knew, a man who would never have used another person for his own lustful gains." I turned away from his unreadable expression, my chest aching. "I *hate* seeing what you've become, knowing that it's my fault. That I didn't protect you when you needed me the most. That's why I avoid you, why I hate being near you, and why I hate *interacting* with you.

"Mikeal is dead, and now we all have Crispin, with no one to blame but me." With that, I left the room, slamming the door again as I stood in the hall-way. I thought I heard him softly call my name, but I ignored it, quickly heading for Justina's room. My gait slowed as I realized I was approaching my door and I paused as I reached it. I slowly fingered the raven carved into the wood, my anger beginning to fade now that I was no longer near the vampire.

Slowly, I went inside, pausing in the doorway of my dark room. My eyes drifted through the darkness before resting on my vanity against the far wall, just visible with the light from the hallway. Turning on the light near the door, I slowly made my way to my small makeup desk and sat down, looking at the rings scattered on its top. I reached for an ornate jewelry box, opening it to reveal the various jewels and gems that had been gifted to me over the years. My eyes rested on a single ring, the reason I had entered my room and been drawn to the desk. It was nothing more than a simple gold band, but I lifted it up, un-able to help the turmoil it caused in my chest.

'*Are you finally going to move on?*' My sister's con-sciousness suddenly spoke, making me jump in my seat. I grabbed the wooden locket that housed my sister's soul as it grew warm under my shirt, her voice annoyed. *'You can't keep holding onto the past forever.'*

"I know." I gazed into the shining metal and this time, I could see his face, hear his laugh as if no time had passed at all. I looked up into the mirror, seeing the dark-skinned beauty that stared back at me. I was abnormal, never to be accepted as a human or a Supernatural. A prize to some, a threat to others, but he had treated me like a treasure, even once he knew what I was. And I repaid that by allowing him to be killed, allowing him to be turned. "I know, I just..."

'Miss him? You can miss him until you're dead, but it'll never bring him back the way you remember him.' I could hear my sister's disdain as she lectured me, and I closed my eyes as she continued. *'Accept what happened, accept that he's changed and stop torturing yourself.'*

"Yeah... I know, I know." I carefully put the ring back where it belonged and, choosing a different one, slowly stood up from my desk. "Go back to sleep, you shouldn't waste energy right now. He knows now, so I'll... I'll be fine."

'Fine. Be well, Raiven.' I quietly left my room as her consciousness faded and I continued to Justina's room. The room was already dark when I stepped inside, and I could hear Justina's soft breathing as she slept. Once inside the dark room, the weight of my day pressed on me, and I felt exhausted as I walked to her bed. Collapsing on top of the sheets next to her, I fell asleep quickly, wishing for the day to end.

3

I awoke late the next day with Justina's strong arms around me and her cool breath on my neck. The scent of vanilla wafted up my nostrils and I quickly realized the being beside me wasn't Justina. I quickly sat up and Aurel laughed as he released me, his grin bright on his face.

"Well, good afternoon. I thought you were going to sleep all day." He sat up as well, revealing that he was shirtless from the waist up. I merely grunted as I rubbed the sleep from my eyes, realizing I was still on top of the sheets. I felt Aurel gently touch my hand, and I allowed him to take it as he spoke. "By the way, I like the ring. It's gorgeous on your petite hands. Whoever got it for you picked it exactly right."

Aurel was studying the band intently, and I couldn't help my slight smile at his fascination. One of Aurel's many hobbies was to collect jewelry from the past and he had quite the collection. After all, he had been collecting for the past hundred years and was jealous of every piece I owned. After a while, he spoke again, the awe obvious in his tone. "This is a

classic, the setting and cut of the stone is iconic. Re-
naissance?"

"Yeah, a good friend got it for me for one of my
birthdays." I smiled, loving Aurel's expression as he
studied the ring. I glanced around the room for its
owner but saw no sign of her. "Where's Justina?"

"Dunno." He shrugged, looking up and releasing
my hand. "She left and told me to watch you. Made
me promise like I'm a fucking gack."

"So, you decided to climb in bed with me?" I joked
as he laughed, unable to help the slight smile that
came to my face. I considered Aurel another of the
few friends I had in the Coven, but lately, things had
become strained between us. Any moment when we
could enjoy being friends was a nice reminder of
what I wanted to preserve. However, as soon as his
laughter began to fade, a soft look entered his eyes
and my smile immediately faded.

"Raiven." He reached to stroke my cheek and I
pulled back, not wanting him to touch me. Aurel's
feelings toward me had begun to shift and while he
had yet to ask me to join his harem, he made no small
secret of how he felt. I didn't feel anything more than
friendship for him and I drew in a deep breath,
steeling myself for what I knew I needed to say.

"Aurel, you need to stop." I stated plainly,
watching as confusion flitted across his face. I was
sure if he had been alive, his face would have changed
color, but being undead left his face the same pale
color. Those gentle sea-green eyes were starting to
show hints of Aurel's annoyance, and I swallowed as I
waited for him to respond.

"Stop what, *A ghrá*[1]?"

"That, right there. You need to stop," I insisted,

finally standing from the bed as he looked after me curiously. My heart pounded as I met his gaze, but I forced myself to meet it evenly. Aurel was playing stupid, but I knew he understood what I meant. Dragging this out wouldn't help either of us, and I couldn't keep my silence. "We're friends, Aurel. I don't want—"

"Want what, Raiven?" Aurel stood, his eyes glowing dangerously as he let his emotions get the better of him. His curly orange hair almost seemed to expand in his annoyance, but I refused to be intimidated, crossing my arms as he stood across from me. I knew Aurel did not take rejection well, but I would not be coerced. "You only spend time with me when you're forced to be here, so why do you put up with me at all? Is there something you're hiding from me?"

"Maybe because I don't want to hurt you, you idiot!" I snorted, moving away from the bed to Justina's armchair. I gripped the back tightly as I scowled at the lich, my own annoyance growing. "Does forcing yourself on me make you any better? Maybe the reason I don't spend time with you is because you always guilt trip me about it. Sometimes you act no better than Mother, wanting to add me to another of your collections."

Surprised flitted across Aurel's face and I immediately regretted my words as I realized what I said. Comparing anyone to Mater Vitae was a great insult, and the words had flown out of my mouth without thought. Upon recognizing the hurt and anger in his eyes, I tried to apologize, releasing the chair as I spoke.

"Aurel, I'm sorry, I didn't—"

"Of course not. You never do." He walked by me without looking up and pushed his way past Crispin and Justina as they walked in the door. I collapsed down into the chair, cradling my face between my hands as I mentally chastised myself for my hasty words. Justina looked after Aurel as he left, turning a quizzical expression to me.

"What did you do?"

"We had a fight, what does it look like?" I replied sarcastically, sighing heavily as I tried to calm myself down. Getting upset with Justina would get me nowhere and I knew it. I looked up from my hands, glancing at the pair as they watched me with concern. "Why did you leave me with him, anyway?"

"I needed to get Crispin up and I was trying to be nice for once. Plus, I thought you... well, obviously I was wrong." Justina shook her head disapprovingly as I tried to change the subject.

"What did you need to get Crispin up for?"

"That's private." She glanced at him and I didn't like the look they shared, frowning as I dropped my hands from my face. It not only confused me, but it was as if they had a whole conversation with that one look. I knew Justina was Second in the Coven, but it wasn't like either of them to keep secrets. Both were honest to a fault, and it caused them both issues with other members of the Coven in their own ways.

"Is there something I should know about?" I didn't do much to hide the suspicion in my voice as I spoke, pulling my legs into the chair. "I'm going to guess it isn't a Coven matter."

"No, nothing like that," Crispin answered, a little too quickly. I decided not to push it as he continued, still giving him an annoyed look. "I know we have permissions for excursions, but we have to be back before LeAlexende and Lucius wake up."

"And? I care because?" I glanced at the clock above her bathroom, which read a little after one. Justina must've used her magic to wake Crispin early and I glanced at her, trying to judge her intention. She was looking away from me, her expression unreadable as she refused to meet my gaze.

"And, I want to show you something." Crispin smiled mysteriously, and Justina looked up to shoot him an angry glance. I didn't even hesitate with my answer.

"No."

"Raiven, please." Crispin looked ready to argue when Justina stopped him and looked at me, a pleading look in her eyes as she spoke first. I turned to face the sorcerer fully, trying to understand her motives. Justina usually tried to stay on an even footing with everyone in the Coven, especially since her anger and her honest mouth often got her in trouble. I couldn't understand why she was supporting whatever Crispin wanted, but since it was her, I decided I was curious enough to find out why.

"Fine. Just leave while I change."

"Sure." Justina cut Crispin off and pushed him out the door, not giving the vampire a chance to annoy me. I grabbed some clothing that I knew I had left in Justina's room, but I decided to dress near the door so I could hear their conversation. Justina's door never closed all the way, due to a fight she got into with a suitor, and Lucius didn't consider it important to repair anymore. She was constantly breaking it for some reason or another, and I couldn't blame him for not wanting to waste the time.

"Don't play with her, Cris. I mean it," Justina warned, her voice low and heavy, almost as if she were preparing to cast. "You'll pay for it. She'll make sure you do and so will I. You just need to tell her the truth."

"I won't play with her." The vampire promised lightly, and it took all I had not to scoff, lest they hear me. Justina sighed heavily and I heard the door groan as she leaned against it slightly.

"You will, I know it," she sounded defeated, and I leaned forward to hear her next words better. "You will never change."

"And you'll never trust me. You know I don't mess around when it's serious... well, not too much." Crispin laughed softly and it sounded like he moved closer to her. "Let me have at least a little fun, Raiven makes it too easy."

Justina never got to reply because I opened the door at that moment and Crispin quickly stepped back. I frowned, still not trying to hide my displeasure and annoyance with having to spend time with the vampire. "I'm as ready as I'll ever be."

"Good." He quickly linked my arm in his and we walked down the dark Coven hallway into the way-too-bright sunshine. At first I thought he might be annoyed by being forced to deal with the sun, but the vampire seemed just fine as he strolled through the parking lot. He was in no danger from it considering his age, but he still preferred to avoid direct sunlight after being out of it for so long. I watched as he produced keys from his pocket, and I looked at the vampire as if he had grown a new head.

"Since when do you drive?"

"Since Justina said I could drive her car and we don't have the time to walk there," Crispin shrugged, unlocking the vehicle to locate where it was in the parking lot. He glanced back to my smug expression, not trying to hide his own annoyance for once. "I know how to drive, Raiven. I just don't see the point in owning a car."

"Yeah, why own a car when you can be undead and responsible and walk?" I muttered sarcastically as I climbed in the car, waiting impatiently as he joined me. Crispin was far from the only undead who preferred to walk most places, but it was easier to be of that opinion when all the trappings of being alive weren't a problem. "Where are we going, anyway?"

"What fun would that be?" He leaned over and kissed my forehead before I could react. After it occurred to me that this was strike three for him, I slapped him, growling slightly. He actually had the audacity to grin at my retaliation, and I realized he'd kissed me to see if he could get a reaction.

"You must have enjoyed it to slap me that hard."

Seething and resisting the desire to slap him again, I turned away from him as we left The Landing. As my anger passed, my mind floated to Aurel and guilt gripped my mind and chest as I remembered my words. It was the worst thing I could've said, considering all the horrible things Mother had done when she controlled Supernaturals and those in her court. Regardless of my lack of romantic feelings and his bad attitude, he hadn't done anything to warrant that kind of comparison.

"Where are we?" I leaned forward as we pulled into what appeared to be a public garden and my confusion continued to grow. Such gardens were common, making it easier for people to plant and care for their own plot of flowers or vegetables, but I couldn't understand why Crispin would take me to one. The vampire merely smiled, getting out and leaning on the car as he waited for me to join him.

"Just set your watch for two-fifteen so we don't end up being late." He still refused to answer my question as he started for the garden's entrance. I set my watch and, leaning against the car, watched him walk away. He managed to get pretty far before he realized I wasn't following, and I couldn't help my smirk as he sighed. "C'mon, Raiven."

"Why?"

"You'll see." He stood there facing me, arms crossed as he turned around. Stubborn, I equally crossed mine and stared at him, refusing to budge. We remained that way for a while and I took a moment to glance at my watch. If I could hold him for a few more minutes, I wouldn't have to worry about whatever it was he wanted to show me. Then suddenly, he tossed his hair, flashing a stream of gold in the sunlight. "Oh well, let's go. I'll just tell Justina that we drove here for nothing."

I was intrigued by his mention of Justina but refused to move for a moment, just to pay him back for earlier. Crispin waited to see if his words had affected me before he started walking towards the car, shaking his head. I waited until he was within arm's length before I walked past him, twisting so he couldn't touch me.

"I knew you'd give in." He grinned behind me as he followed and I shrugged, pretending not to care.

"It's not always about you," I warned, opening the garden's gate. "I only gave in because if I didn't, it would've been a waste for Justina and unlike how I feel about you, I like her."

"True, true." He nodded, only pretending to agree.

I turned around and slapped him again – half for the sarcasm I didn't appreciate, half because he was so cocky. He reached to grab my hand but I was quick to snatch it back, hissing as he walked past me. I growled as I began following him, wanting this outing to be over with.

'*Raiven.*' My sister's voice rose in my mind again as she responded to my annoyance. '*Who are you with?*'

'*Say hello to the new improved Mikael, now known as Crispin.*' The locket grew warm under my shirt and out of habit, I reached up to grab it. Once I realized Crispin was watching me, however, I stopped. '*Stay low, sis, or you'll be discovered again and this bastard is the last person I want to find out.*'

'*If you don't want to be with him anymore, then leave. No need to get so worked up.*' I began to refute her statement but she slipped away before I could respond. I looked up as Crispin moved aside a curtain of beads and he motioned me in as I marveled at the beauty of the garden. It was filled with a variety of flowers, all of which were beautifully in bloom. However, it was more than that: it was my garden, a garden I had tended to what seemed like a lifetime ago.

"I knew you'd like it." My awe immediately faded and I turned to glare as Crispin spoke. He raised his hands in defense and he seemed strangely sincere. "Not like that: you used to have a garden like this, I'm pretty sure. It's where I pro... was going to propose. Never mind, that's not what's important."

Crispin came closer to me and I instinctively stepped back, growling softly at him. He sighed heavily, stepping back as he looked away. All of his usual playfulness was gone from his eyes and he gingerly touched one of the petals, looking at it softly before returning his gaze to me. For a brief moment, he was like his old self again, gleaming in the sunlight as he helped care for a garden he thought so dutifully reflected me.

"I planted this a few years before you came. I'm not much for gardens now, and I didn't really know why, but I just felt compelled to. Justina... helps me with it," his newly softened expression looked strange to me, as if it didn't belong to him. The man standing in front of me seemed more like Mikael than Crispin and I couldn't help but step closer to him, my heart filling with an ache I thought I no longer had. "I know you probably don't believe me when I say this, but... I do appreciate you telling me. I don't remember and I probably never will, but–"

Crispin moved quickly and wrapped his arms around me, holding me close. Before I could object or react, he leaned down and kissed me, but this no longer felt like Crispin. I couldn't help myself as I wrapped my arms around him to pull him closer, my heart aching as I did so. I had never forgiven myself for allowing Mikael to be turned and never realized how much I still missed him. His gentle, uncertain kisses, the soft tenderness of being in his arms... and blood. His lips had the tainted taste of blood and now I tasted it faintly through the kiss. My mental cage to keep my thirst at bay started to break down as I kissed him deeply to taste more of that sweet liquid.

"Raiven." His voice was muffled from the force I was now pushing on him, almost forcing him to the ground. He tried his best to shift his arms to push me away, but I tightened my grip to keep him still. I was starting to lose my grasp on where I was and who I was with; all that mattered was the blood in his mouth and getting more of it. I pulled away from his lips and started for his throat, my fangs extending from my mouth.

"Raiven!" Crispin managed to untangle himself from me and pushed me into a bed of flowers, the gentle blooms crushed by my fall. "What in hell is wrong with you?"

I almost sprang back up, wanting more, but his push allowed me to regain enough control to slam the addiction behind its steel doors. I breathed in the scent of the flowers to calm myself as the lusty glow left my eyes and my fangs disappeared back into my mouth.

"Sorry," I muttered, somewhat embarrassed as I stood. "It has been a while since... since I've lost control like that... and it's almost time, so—"

"I know." The cockiness was still gone, replaced by a kind man. At least, he still looked less cocky and more concerned. "We have to stay away from you when we have injuries, but I haven't been hurt. Not recently, anyway."

"The faintest taste was still there." A glow began in my eyes as I thought about the kiss, but I pushed it back. "It's been months since Lucius fed me, and the mere thought of undead blood is enough to set me off. Such a soft, sweet—"

"Look, Raiven. I'm sorry." He breathed and I was so surprised by it that it overcame the addiction that had tried to take over my mind again. Crispin didn't apologize, not even to Lucius and definitely not to a woman. "I didn't bring you out here to play with you, despite what you may think. Honestly, I need..."

Crispin paused, looking away from me, pouting at

a bed of white hibiscus flowers. I wasn't sure what to make of what was happening as I looked over the vampire, doing my best to ignore my thirst. Crispin turned back as if he was finally ready to speak when my watch began to scream, startling us both. It started a shriek that would have made a banshee proud as the alarm went off, declaring the time loudly.

Glancing at Crispin, I left the garden and began for the car, nearly running as we went. Crispin was faster and reached it first, quickly sliding into the driver's seat and I didn't argue as I jumped in. Whether I wanted to or not, we had to return to The Dream before Lucius and LeAlexende woke up for the day or the Oath would punish us both. As Crispin sped us back, I couldn't help but wonder what he had wanted to say in the recreated garden.

4

I leaned against my car as Crispin walked into the
Coven, disappearing past the barrier into the
darkness below. If we walked in together, it
would've raised so many unnecessary problems with
Eve that I didn't want to deal with. I could be a smar-
tass when I wanted to, but I preferred to just avoid
the ala as much as possible.

As I waited, my mind drifted back to the garden
and I didn't like the uncomfortable feeling it caused
in my chest. He had seemed... too different from what
I had come to expect from him and his demeanor left
me confused. Sincerity was not in Crispin's vocabu-
lary and I had never seen him be so soft with anyone.
A part of me wanted to believe that Mikael was still in
him somewhere, but another argued that he was no
longer that person. I had always agreed with the lat-
ter, but now, I wasn't sure what to think.

A few minutes after Crispin disappeared, Aurel
came storming up the stairs, slamming the door into
the wall. Barely glancing my way, he smashed his fist
into the concrete, cursing in a language I didn't know.

He had still failed to put on a shirt apparently, his alabaster skin practically blinding in the afternoon sunlight.

"Aurel!" I tried to get his attention, my pride screaming at me as I did so. If looks could kill, I would've died ten times over from the glare he gave me. I frowned, displeased with his reaction. "What the fuck's your problem?"

"What's my problem?" Suddenly he was in my face and vanilla flooded my mind until I wanted to push him back before the sweet scent suffocated me. "Oh, nothing, just that Eve is being a fucking annoying scanger!"

"Well, sorry, that's not really news around here." I didn't like him taking his anger out on me, especially when I had nothing to do with it. Most of us thought Evalyn abused her position as Lucius' Retainer, but that was hardly my fault. I realized Eve probably had taken a jab at Aurel's harem again, something he was very protective about. "*I* was trying to apologize."

The angry lines left his face, but he didn't move, his orange curls bouncing. He looked at me with genuine confusion as he spoke, still leaning over me. "Apologize for what?"

"What I said earlier," I muttered, looking away. "I didn't mean to say it like that or to compare you to Mother. I don't really think you're like her. You're... pushy at times, but you do genuinely care about others. Like with your harem, and that's something she could never understand."

He seemed surprised for a moment before smiling at me, putting his hands on my car, and pinning me to the hood with his body. Aurel leaned down as if to kiss me and I turned away from him. He instead placed a light kiss on my cheek, lips barely brushing against my skin. He pulled back slightly, his eyes now looking at me softly.

"Don't worry about it. I'm over it." Aurel grinned at me and I chuckled softly, gently pushing him back. He let me, still standing as close as he could.

"While I'm glad, it doesn't change what I said before that," I insisted, watching as his smile twitched. I sighed, crossing my arms as I met his eyes evenly. "We're just friends, Aurel."

"What can I say? Things change all the time." He grinned, leaning back over me as he moved to hug me. As he brought his hand to caress my face, I could smell the blood on his knuckles and I had to shove him away. After my encounter with Crispin, my addiction was already barely under control and I looked at him with horror. He looked at me surprised, confused by my refusal of him. "What's wrong?"

"You just injured yourself. You need to leave." I turned away from him, trying not to think about the blood now running through his veins. The black, sweet blood that filled his luscious body, waiting for me to indulge. I grabbed my arm as it shot out to grab him, digging my nails into my own skin. "You need to leave now. You know better than to come around me like that."

"Raiven." His voice whined with how much he wanted to stay, but I knew it wasn't safe for either of us. I shook my head, refusing to look at him.

"Leave now, Aurel, or I *will* make you leave. Don't come near me until you've healed." I found it difficult to speak as my fangs tried to reveal themselves and I fought to keep them in my mouth. After a long, silent pause, I heard Aurel walk away and breathed a sigh of relief as the door to the Coven closed. I opened my eyes to the afternoon sun and tried to control my blood lust.

"You okay, Rai?" I looked down to see Kisten step out of his silver Mustang. He was dressed up with a blue silk shirt and black dress pants, and a simple gold chain around his neck. His hair was combed back into a slick-back style, with a few strands refusing to obey and hanging in his face. I dug my nails into the hood of my car, the screeching sound almost enough to distract my mind. Every fiber of my being was insisting I descend into the Coven, chase after Aurel to drink his sweet, undead blood.

"Go away, don't come near me," I growled through semi-closed lips and I closed my eyes. I was close to crying as I heard Kisten walk towards me, struggling to keep my body from chasing the lich. If I lost the battle and Kisten tried to stop me, there was no telling what I would do to him, and the last thing I wanted was to hurt him.

Suddenly, I felt a sharp pain in my hand and I opened my eyes to see Kisten piercing my skin with his sharp claws. Kisten was such an old and experienced shifter that he could shift any part of himself that he wanted to and his hand and forearm bore his beautiful leopard spots. Despite the blood his claws were now drawing from me, I felt an urge to pet the soft fur gracing his skin.

Before I could ask why he had stabbed me, Kisten forced my hand to my mouth, allowing me to taste my own blood. As soon as the taste hit my mouth, all thoughts of wanting blood faded. The cold, metallic taste was nothing like the sweet taste I craved and was familiar with. It was like jumping into a cold shower: I sobered up quickly and the addiction faded to its usual dark pit. I looked at Kisten in surprise as he released me, still holding my hand to my mouth, and letting the blood flow in. He smiled at me softly, shifting his hand back to being human.

"You never thought of that?"

"I..." I wanted to give some sort of excuse, but I couldn't think of anything to say. Kisten's eyes lit up with mirth, and I saw the corners of his mouth twitch up as he worked to hold in his laughter. I took my hand out of my mouth, and tried my hardest to look upset, fighting my own smile. "Well, why in the world would I ever do that to myself?"

"It seemed like a good idea. Would be bad if you wanted to drink your own blood." He shrugged, turning to walk back to his car. "Give me a moment to get my kit and I'll treat you."

I said nothing and merely watched as he dug through his trunk to find his first aid kit. As the Alpha of The Capital, Kisten took taking care of all shapeshifters seriously and it was obvious why he and Lucius were both good friends, as well as connected as Overseer and Alpha. His kit was fitted to treat any kind of shapeshifter and almost any possible wound that could be sustained, whether from each other or other Supernaturals.

He came back with a large roll of gauze as well as a needle and thread and I winced when I noticed. Kisten set down the supplies and reached for my hand, but I instinctively pulled it away, looking at the needle. Kisten followed my gaze and gave me an incredulous look.

"Are you seriously about to tell me you are afraid of needles?"

"I'm not afraid, just..." The words faded and Kisten sighed, taking my uninjured hand in his. He gently stroked the back of my hand before quickly kissing it, the gesture burning my skin.

"Uncomfortable? Because of Mother?" he whispered, and I nodded, wanting to press his hand to my face, wishing I could relax in his arms. He kissed the back of my hand again before releasing it and gently touching my face with his fingertips, the closest he would get to caressing me. "You know I know what I'm doing. It'll be a quick stitch and taken out tomorrow once you've healed."

"I know." I closed my eyes as he got to work, doing my best to ignore the sensations. Kisten was a surgeon and worked at the local hospital, specializing in treatment of Supernaturals. It was kind of unfair to his patients, since technically, he oversaw so many of them, but I think it was how Kisten preferred it. Working at the hospital gave him the authority that he needed to take care of his people, no matter the circumstance.

"There, done." Kisten patted my freshly dressed wound and I opened my eyes. Green met chartreuse as we looked at one another and, unable to resist, I reached out to touch his face with my uninjured hand. His hand caught mine however, and he held it awkwardly for a moment, before picking up my bandaged hand and pressing it to his face instead. He kept his eyes locked on mine and I felt as if my heart would beat right out of my chest.

"This isn't what I want." I sighed, dropping my hand in frustration as I looked away. Kisten dropped his as well, gathering up his materials from the hood of my car. He held out his hand and I accepted it as he helped me down.

"I know, Raiven, but I can't hurt you again." Kisten's expression resumed its gloomy stare and my heart sank. It had been a long time since I had allowed anyone into my heart, but Kisten...he was different. Kisten had been so lonely for so long, it was as if he didn't remember what it felt like to be loved by another person. I never went long without physical comfort, but before me was a man who had not touched another being in more than two centuries. I never questioned him about it, but I wanted to know why he had chosen to be by himself for so long.

"C'mon, Raiven, you need to get ready." Kisten's voice drew me from my thoughts and I watched as he checked his shirt for bloodstains. It dawned on me that he wasn't supposed to be at the Coven while LeAlexende was in town and I gave him a confused look.

"Actually, Kisten, why are you here? I thought yo—" I was interrupted by the door behind me slamming open, and I turned to see LeAlexende and Lucius bursting up the stairs, carrying someone between them. Lucius turned to look at us and relief flooded his eyes when he saw Kisten. It was then that I noticed the dark blue hair and the constant dripping blood from my friend's body.

"Kisten, it's Justina, she—" Lucius didn't get to finish as I scooped up my friend from the Overseers and rushed her into the backseat of Kisten's car, sliding in with her. Kisten quickly got into the driver's seat and gave a quick nod to Lucius, who simply nodded back. The other two moved to Lucius' car as Kisten peeled out of the parking lot and sped down the road. As he flew to make it to the hospital, I held Justina's hand tightly. She was still alive, but barely and I prayed that we would make it in time.

5

I waited impatiently in the waiting room with the two Overseers, unable to help my pacing. As soon as we arrived, the staff backed out of Kisten's way, allowing him to place Justina on an empty gurney. They recognized who Justina was immediately and merely rushed him off to surgery, allowing him to choose the doctor who assisted him.

She was badly torn up, almost as if she had been hacked by several blades or slashed many times by claws. All Lucius and LeAlexende could tell me was that they woke up to her screaming and when they tried to enter her room with Crispin, they found themselves unable to open the door. Finally, Crispin used his power to rip the door off its hinges and they found Justina in that state, barely conscious from blood loss. Lucius then ordered Crispin to remain behind and to check on the other spellcasters in the Coven, as well as enlist the help of his Fourth, Liel.

I called my boss as soon as Kisten took Justina into surgery and asked him to bring one of the agents with him to the hospital. Although not a perfect fit, the MO fit our current case a little too well for me to ignore it. I wanted to ask Justina what happened, but I knew that Brandon also needed to hear whatever she might have to say.

"What's the status, Raiven?" Brandon walked into the waiting room with Chris, one of our better agents, in tow. Lucius and Brandon exchanged a cursory nod before my boss turned back to me, doing his best to ignore the Overseer.

"Jus... The victim is currently in surgery. It's Justina, second to Lucius and a powerful...witch in her own right." I tried my best to remain calm and professional as I recounted what the Overseers had told me and Chris dutifully wrote it all down. Brandon sighed heavily after asking a few more questions of the pair, rubbing his temples as he groaned.

"I'll be honest, this is a breakthrough if it's related and she survives," he muttered, stretching his neck. "We've never had a survivor before, although I find it strange that she was alone. Usually, there are multiple people in a room before our suspect attacks, in order to claim as many victims as possible."

"That would be impossible inside the Coven," Lucius offered, and we turned to face him. "Never more than three to a room for extended periods of time, and larger groups must take place in open areas with no doors."

"Why such a rule?"

"Infighting, for one. That many different species in a small space can fuel some century-old tensions," I answered, crossing my arms across my chest as I spoke for Lucius. "But also because of Mo... Mater Vitae."

"You mean the one who made Supernaturals?" Brandon asked and I looked to Lucius to explain. Lucius gave me an exasperated glance before returning his attention to my boss. "What does she have to do with groups?"

"If too many Supernaturals gather at once, Mater Vitae can... manifest if she wants, due to all of us carrying her blood," Lucius explained cautiously and it was obvious from his tone that he didn't want to talk about it. "She... is not favorable to have around, so most Overseers have similar rules."

"Hmmm, explains why many of the murders included quite a number of humans..." Chris mused, flipping through his notebook. "But what role do Supernaturals play in his choice of victims? He doesn't seem to be going after a certain species, just numbers. But then, why would he go after Justina on her own?"

"Unless..." An idea started into my head and I didn't like where my thoughts were leading me. "They knew what she was and wanted to take her out first."

"What she was? She's a witch, isn't she?" Brandon gave me a strange look and Lucius' eyes lit up with worry. He almost seemed to be panicked, an expression I was not used to seeing on his face. LeAlexende gently touched his back, giving a friendly rub as the vampire spoke.

"No. No one could know that," he stammered and looked between his hands to the floor. It wasn't like Lucius to let his composure fall like that, but I understood his distress well. "We've never told anyone, no one knows except for members of the Coven."

"Know what?" Brandon asked again, clearly confused and getting frustrated as LeAlexende did his best to comfort his friend. I looked to Lucius for confirmation and he met my eyes with worry. I understood his concern, but I needed to explain everything to Brandon.

'It could help us catch the one who did this.' I mouthed to him behind my boss, not even trying to hide my anger. Brandon didn't know I was anything more than human, so I couldn't let him know that Lucius was anything more to me than a friend. However, as Justina's power was a Coven secret, I couldn't say it without permission. Lucius' brow furrowed but he nodded, covering his face with his hands again.

"Justina isn't a witch. She's a sorcerer," I started, breathing deeply, and Brandon and Chris looked at me, waiting for me to continue. "She can cast both without a wand and silently."

"Mental casting?" Chris exclaimed, both shocked and excited and a sharp look from me made him lower his voice. "But the implications of that are huge! Magic is shaped by the sound of a spellcasters' voice and focused through a medium. To be able to cast without doing that would change everything we know about them and–"

"Would make them more dangerous." Brandon nodded, deep in thought. "It makes sense that it would be kept a secret. I'd imagine other spellcasters would not welcome someone like that."

"No, sorcerers often hide their abilities," I answered softly. "But for our suspect to know that, means they must've known Justina before she came to The Capital. I've known Justina for a while and she told me and now, everyone in this room knows."

I shot a glare at Chris and the sullen look on his face and his uncomfortable gulp made it clear that my point had gotten across. I might have needed to share the information for the sake of finding her attacker, but I was not willing to put her life in danger if others found out what she was.

"So, if his plan was to take Justina out so she couldn't cast without him knowing," LeAlexende spoke, his voice soft as he contributed to the conversation. "Doesn't that mean that he hasn't actually committed his crime yet?"

"Shit, he's right!" Brandon cursed, starting to pace as I had done earlier. "Which means he is choosing his Supernatural victims to some extent... he has to be if he knows what they're capable of. That supports the elf theory, but god, that's a lot of work for a bugger like that."

"I'll get the rest of the team on conference and we'll go through each of the previous victims again with this new outlook. Maybe we can find something similar with the other killings before he tries to go for his actual kill." Brandon nodded to Chris and the agent turned to leave the waiting room. "You stay here and call me if she wakes up. Keep me updated on her progress. I don't want to press her if she makes it through, but... if she knew someone who could do this, we could finally stop this lunatic."

"I know." I nodded and Brandon rushed to join Chris, the two talking among themselves. Soon after my boss and coworker disappeared, Kisten came in, pushing Justina's bed into the waiting room. Kisten held the door open as they moved her into a proper room and closed the door as the other doctor went inside to finish getting her set up. As soon as we were alone, Lucius leapt to his feet, clearly worried.

"Kis–"

"She's alive." We all sighed with relief at his words and waited for him to continue. Kisten pulled his gloves off his hands, refusing to look at any of us. "But it is bad. We did what we could, gave her a transfusion, but whoever it was, they were clearly attempting to kill her. She's unlikely to wake up for a few days."

"But she's alive, and she'll survive?" Lucius asked cautiously, clearly preparing himself for a harsh response. Kisten sighed, running his hand through his dark hair as he hesitated with his answer. I wanted to hug him, to squeeze his hand and tell him he had done all that he could, but knew how impossible that was. Lucius walked towards the Alpha, his voice soft. "Kisten?"

"It depends on her. She suffered no major organ damage and it seems like she's been casting a healing spell on herself unconsciously, but considering her age..." Kisten admitted, dropping his hand back to his side as he shook his head. "We stitched up her large gashes and set her bones so that they heal properly, so—"

"Wait, she had broken bones?" I interrupted, my tone incredulous, and Kisten nodded, giving me a strange look.

"Yeah, both of her legs were broken as well..." I turned around to call my boss as Kisten watched me, confused. I heard Lucius explaining to him about my case as my phone rang and Brandon could barely squeeze out a hello before I interrupted him.

"Put me on the call," I demanded and resumed as soon as I could hear the background noise of my other co-workers. "She has broken bones. Both legs."

"Broken bones? Well, that kills the elf theory." My female coworker, Julia, sounded disappointed. "I mean, an elf killing a witch is ludicrous to begin with, but a cunning Dokkalfar could've pulled it off."

"Yeah, but neither Ljosalfar or Dokkalfar would have the inhuman strength needed to break a bone that quickly," Chris spoke, and it sounded like he was still writing on his notepad. I motioned for the two Overseers and Kisten to be silent and carefully put my phone on speaker. "Meaning there's really only two species who can both overcome a magic barrier spell and still possess inhuman strength to snap leg bones."

"Harpies and Cyclops, right?" Brandon offered and I noticed Kisten shook his head, holding up his index finger. I spoke quickly, looking at him, confused.

"Actually, there's one more." Kisten scrambled to the waiting room table and began to write something on one of the magazines. I could hear the disbelief of my colleagues as I waited to see what Kisten wanted to tell me.

"What? We ruled gargoyles out a long time ago and elves just got ruled out," another one of my team-mates, Justin, spoke up. "If not harpies or cyclops, then what?"

Kisten finally finished his writing and the name caused a chill to run up my spine. I knew what they were, but I was uncomfortable saying the name out loud, and I understood why he didn't want to, either.

"An empousa." I whispered and the background noise grew deadly silent on both ends of the phone, no one daring to breathe after I said the word out loud. I almost expected Mater Vitae to appear right then, but luckily, no such thing happened as we waited. Quietly, Chris started to whisper on his end with Brandon.

"But... aren't they extinct? I thought they were wiped out by Hunters a long time ago."

"Even with the tell of a copper limb, it would be hard to be sure of that," Justin reasoned. "It is completely possible that a few could've survived and are in hiding to avoid Hunters."

"But records of empousa are scarce, we barely know anything about them and even if we knew more, it's not like any would be registered in our system." Brandon sighed heavily, clearly not happy. "Dammit, every clue we get sets us back more. Raiven, ask Lucius if there is anything he could tell us about these empousa, including if he ever knew any. Meanwhile, we'll keep looking into any connections the other victims could have with Justina. Knowing the species is good and all, but does us no good if we can't find the fucker."

"Will do." I agreed and waited until he hung up before turning to Lucius. He had an unreadable expression on his face and was looking away out the window. I moved to speak, but Kisten stopped me, shaking his head. He stared after Lucius with a painful look on his face and LeAlexende was also pensive.

"One of my former Retainers was an Empousa," Lucius breathed and a pit immediately formed in my stomach as I understood the implication. "But she wouldn't have known about Justina. She... was hunted long before I even crossed the sea. I–"

"Lucius." I stopped him, placing my hand on his shoulder. After a moment, he softly touched it, giving me a slight squeeze. "I'm sorry."

54

"It's alright, it was my own weakness that allowed Plumeria to be taken from me." Lucius' voice darkened as he continued. "We will not lose Justina to anyone."

"No, we won't," I agreed, stepping away as he released me. I turned back to face Kisten, who was still pensive. "I am more than a little concerned about our culprit possibly being an empousa. I won't say he doesn't have reason to want to attack other Supernaturals, but the Hunters wiped them out, not the community."

"Hunters were ordered by Mother to eradicate them, but they certainly had a lot of help from others," Kisten sighed, shaking his head as he took off his coat and I noticed the blood on his shirt. He must've started surgery before donning his coat; it was probably the other doctor who had forced him to wear it. He folded it over his arm as he continued. "Shapeshifters have always been treated poorly among Supernaturals. I'd imagine many of them were given up to the Hunters once Mother decided to eradicate them."

"But none of our victims have been known to work with Hunters, current or former," I remarked, and Kisten raised his eyebrows. I shrugged, folding my arms across my chest. "Just seemingly random, unless he's hunting those who are related to others who ratted out empousa to the Hunters."

"Then he would have no reason to be here," Lucius sneered, clearly upset. "Most of my current Coven came after I crossed the sea. Beyond a few, none of them would've known about Plumeria."

"It's okay, Lucius. We'll figure this out." I spoke softly as he turned to face me, his expression still blank. "This is what I do. We didn't have a chance to prevent the other killings, but we won't allow him to kill on our own turf. This is as personal to my team as it is to us, trust me on that."

"I do," Lucius stated plainly, and LeAlexende sighed, finally turning our attention to him. He had remained silent during most of our exchange and I had almost forgotten he was with us. Lucius' expression changed, smiling wryly. "I'm sorry, Alex, but I must ask that you shorten your visit."

"Unnecessary, I'm here to help." LeAlexende's tone was strange as he turned to look at me, a soft smile still on his face. "Raiven, can you tell me where and when all the other killings occurred? I have connections to determine if an empousa was present in any of those areas."

"Connections?" I queried and he nodded, refusing to say more. I was suspicious, but Lucius nodded and gave me a silent order. I knew better than to argue and merely turned to Kisten. "Do you have anywhere I can get actual paper?"

"Yeah, follow me." As I followed Kisten out of the waiting room, I could hear the two friends whispering behind us.

6

"What do you make of this, Kisten?" I leaned back in his chair as I finished writing down the list LeAlexende had asked for. Kisten had taken me to his office, which was down the hallway from Justina's room. The office was pristine and immaculate, not a single paper or pen out of place. It reflected the personality that Kisten projected so perfectly: calm, clean and under control.

Kisten remained quiet and seemed to be deep in thought; He had barely moved as I finished writing my list, staring at one of the many charts in his office. I sighed at his lack of a response, allowing myself to spring forward in the office chair.

"That something still isn't right," he spoke, shaking his head and surprising me with his voice. "It's too convenient. Empousas were hunted centuries ago, so if your suspect was an empousa, why risk exposure like this? And why include humans at all, why not just kill individual Supernaturals? Why kill so many if they aren't the target?"

"I know, and you're not wrong. That's been the

57

whole problem with this case." I closed my eyes, thinking of the previous crime scene. A high school gym, the scene of a prom gone horribly wrong. I still remembered walking into the side room where the murders took place and a shiver ran through me. "It would be incredibly risky and stupid, but if they are a new generation who wasn't adequately taught about Mother, they might try something like this because they can."

"It just seems unlikely it would be an empousa."

"I get that, but then who and why?" I leaned forward on his desk, cradling my head. "It's been my biggest headache. There's no obvious motive, nothing that strings all these victims together. Brandon said it best: the more we learn, the less this all makes sense. Every new crime kills any previous theory."

"So, an empousa is your best lead at the moment." Kisten leaned against his desk and I stood, touching his arm. He absently placed his hand on mine, sighing again. "I don't like this. It feels like we're missing the writing on the wall."

"Don't I know it." I stepped closer to him, releasing his arm, and reaching for his face. He instinctively stopped me, grabbing my wrist without even looking up to me. I grunted, annoyed by his reaction.

"You know you can't." He closed his eyes, refusing to look at me. His grip on my hand tightened for a moment before he relaxed his hold. "I can't keep giving in to—"

"Please," I pleaded, and Kisten looked up to see my face. As our eyes met, I could finally see just how hard this was on him and Kisten's worry for both Justina and Lucius was plain on his face. He once told me that Lucius was like a quiet beehive: if you left it alone and didn't try to knock it over, everything was fine. However, the moment a member of the colony was hurt, the whole swarm would never leave you alone until you paid for your crime.

Kisten slowly released my hand, and I softly touched his face, at first only allowing my fingertips to touch his skin. Even with such a soft gesture, Kisten purred slightly and leaned into my hand, clearly showing how much he craved my touch. My chest ached at the sight of my skin against his; the contrast of my dark skin against his tan complexion always made my heart skip a beat.

Taking a deep breath, I placed my whole hand against his cheek and as he sighed his contentment, I hissed with pain. My whole hand felt like it was burning and the longer I held my hand to his face, the more my body screamed with pain. It traveled down my arm and I pulled it away as the heat reached my chest. I held my aching arm and Kisten quickly grabbed my shoulder, causing me to wince. He loosened his grip, lightly stroking my short sleeve.

"Are you alright? It didn't hurt too badly?" I shook my head as I forced a smile, releasing my still aching arm. He looked at me with concern and my heart began pounding in my chest.

"I'm fine, Kisten. I just wanted to give you some comfort." I smiled as I looked into his eyes and I reached up to touch his face again. This time, he grabbed my arm, stopping me long before I could touch his skin.

"Don't tempt me like this, Raiven," he pleaded, his voice high-pitched as he closed his eyes. My heart pounded from his words, but I remained silent. He slowly opened his eyes, turning his gloomy gaze to me. "I don't want to hurt you anymore."

"You're not, the Oath is," I scoffed, pulling my arm away and Kisten looked as if he wanted to reach for me, but he stopped himself. I reached for him instead, hugging him tightly as I kept my arms on his shirt. He grew still under my touch before gently wrapping his arms around me, careful not to touch my bare skin. I dropped my head into his chest, sighing heavily with my frustration. "It isn't your fault and I would never blame you."

"It *is* my fault," Kisten leaned down, careful to lay his head on my shoulder and to avoid touching my neck. This was as intimate as he would allow us to get and the most he had touched me in more than a year. Any more, and the Oath of Loyalty would ensure that I paid the price. "I should've had Lucius release me from the Oath a long time ago."

"Why didn't you?" I asked tentatively, my voice soft and quiet. Kisten grew still again, and I regretted my question as we remained in silence for a long time, holding each other. I tightened my grip around him and after a moment, he sighed, returning my gesture.

"It didn't matter to me at the time," he spoke softly and slowly, his breath warm against my skin. I felt my heart pound, moving into my throat as he leaned into me more, almost standing from his desk. "I... never thought I'd find someone I wanted like this."

"You mean you've never been with anyone?" I pushed him back, looking at him incredulously. He looked away from me, slightly blushing and I couldn't help the accusing smile that started on my face.

"Kisten, you're over three hundred years old, and you're telling me you've never been with anyone?"

"It's not like I never wanted to," he retorted, still blushing at my teasing and I let out a small giggle at his reaction. It faded when he turned to face me, his eyes filled with loss. "I just... couldn't ever be with them and I... gave up when they finally died. I felt like I had died."

"I-I'm sorry, Kisten." I started to pull away from him, but he kept his arms wrapped around me, still careful not to touch my skin. I could feel his breath against my face and for a moment, I thought he was going to kiss me and despite how painful I knew it would be, my heart pounded at the thought. Instead, I felt him dig his hands into my side, pulling at the fabric of my shirt.

"Don't be," he whispered, his breath hot and heavy as he breathed his words against my skin, allowing his breath to caress me. His hands gripped me tightly through my clothing and I was slightly surprised by his actions. Kisten always maintained an incredibly careful and calm demeanor, always distancing himself from me when he thought he was losing control. He growled softly, his voice sounding animalistic. "You're all that I want now."

A sudden knock at his door made him release me, and we quickly pulled away from each other. Kisten closed his eyes for a moment as I tried to smooth out my shirt. The shifter adjusted himself, settling into a more comfortable position against his desk.

"Come in," he called out and the door opened to LeAlexende, who quietly stepped into the office. The Overseer had a solemn expression, still perturbed by what he had witnessed at the Coven. He closed the door slowly, still lost in thought as he looked at the floor.

"Is your list ready?" LeAlexende slowly looked up, carefully glancing between me and Kisten. It was clear he suspected something from the look he finally gave me and, clearing my throat, I reached to the desk and handed him the paper.

"Yes, it is. All the known killings that have been attributed to our suspect and their locations." I said as he glanced it over, nodding as he folded it. "I hope it's useful."

"Me too. I'll start as soon as I get settled in Justina's room." Kisten nodded solemnly at the Overseer's words. "Lucius has asked that I remain to watch her while I reach out to my contacts. I will give both of you a call if and when her condition changes."

"Thank you, LeAlexende. For everything." Kisten bowed his head to the Overseer, and after a moment, I followed. LeAlexende merely smiled as he waved us off, his expression somewhat like his previous cheery nature.

"You and Lucius are good friends of mine. This is just as personal to me as it is to you," I gave Kisten a questioning look as the Overseer turned to leave, but he either didn't notice or was ignoring me. LeAlexende paused in the doorway, barely glancing over his shoulder to talk to us. "Oh, by the way, Lucius wants all of the Coven in pairs from now on. You two are to stay together at all times, at least until the culprit is caught."

Both Kisten and I stood shocked as LeAlexende made his way out, closing the door behind him. My heart was pounding as I stared at the closed door, my mind still trying to process what I had heard. Slowly, we turned to look at each other before Kisten bolted to his door, walking out of it with me shortly behind. Kisten walked up to Lucius just as Eve walked out of the elevator into the waiting room.

"Lucius," Kisten called his name plainly, and Lucius turned to face us as Eve settled herself in his lap. Eve shot both of us an angry glance before snuggling up to Lucius and, as usual, her display made me want to gag. Kisten ignored Eve entirely as he continued speaking. "Why am I paired with Raiven? Wouldn't it make more sense for me to be with you? Or even Evalyn?"

"Eve will be with me," Lucius stated matter-of-factly, wrapping his arm around his Retainer. It wasn't uncommon for Overseers to be romantically involved with their Retainer or Alpha, or both in some cases. Despite most of the Coven disliking her, we had no choice but to accept Lucius' decision until she died, or he replaced her. "There isn't anyone else I can pair you with, power-wise. Liel and Crispin are paired, I have Aurel with Grace and Yoreile is with Quinn. Everyone else is out of the area and—"

"Problem, Kisten?" Eve asked innocently and both Lucius and Kisten glared at her. Evalyn went out of her way to try and make Kisten miserable, jealous of his long friendship with Lucius. She lacked the understanding that the two weren't involved romantically in any way and continued to perceive him as a rival. Like her jealousy of me, Eve was excellent at overlooking the obvious if she felt someone was standing in her way. "I didn't think you had anything against her."

"I... don't, but..." Kisten stopped himself, holding his head in his hands as I remained silent, since I understood why he didn't want to be paired with me. Kisten had spent the better part of a year keeping me at arm's length, making sure he wouldn't lose his precious control. He took a deep breath as he chose his next words carefully. "I'm not allowed at the Coven. I was only stopping by today because you asked me to prepare dinner. You ordered Raiven to stay."

"Raiven is only as bound as she wants to be." Lucius spoke nonchalantly, Eve leaning her head against his shoulder. "Besides, I'm now ordering her to stay by your side. She'll just have to stay at your house."

My heart was pounding so loud, I could barely feel the order as it passed through me. Stuck at his house, always required to be in the same space as him: it sounded like torture of the cruelest kind! I could barely stand being alone with him for a few hours before I wanted to embrace him, much less days. Kisten certainly knew this, as he continued to argue until Lucius stopped him.

"I've made my decision, Kisten," Lucius narrowed his blue eyes, his hair bristling slightly as he grew annoyed. "Despite my faith in your and Raiven's power, I will not risk having either of you alone. Now, unless you can give me a *valid* reason as to why you cannot be with Raiven, this conversation is over."

Kisten stopped, seeing he could not talk Lucius out of this without telling the truth. He stood still for a moment, and I held my breath, waiting to see what he would do. Finally, he dropped his shoulders, taking a deep breath before turning to face me.

"I'll be right back, then we can go," he muttered, walking past me back down to his office. I was slightly surprised that he wasn't honest; I'd imagine if Eve hadn't been there, he might have been. I was torn between whether I was supposed to follow him or stay, when Lucius called my name.

"Raiven, please." I turned to face him, his cool eyes on me as he stroked Eve's side, my heart aching as I watched. When he spoke again, I forced myself to look away from his hand and to his face. "Take care of him. He won't admit it, but he's not as happy being alone as he says."

Don't I know it. I merely nodded as Kisten returned and walked past me without saying a word. I gave Lucius one final glance as I hurried after him, barely making it to the elevator before the door closed.

7

I silently stared out the window as we drove out of Decver, watching the sky as the sun set beyond the horizon as I sent my text to my pet sitter, asking her to watch my cats for a few more days. As usual, she was more than willing to watch my babies and I hummed softly as I laid my phone in my lap. Kisten was silent and kept his eyes on the road, refusing to even look at me. I knew he was thinking the same thing as me: how long could we deal with this before we both went insane?

My desire for Kisten had been purely physical when we first met; he simply was attractive to me. Dark hair, mysterious eyes, longevity and a cool demeanor that just begged to be broken down. After he told me that he was still bound to Lucius and Eve via the Oath, I had tried to just be his friend after seeing how miserable he truly was. Kisten always kept to himself unless he was needed and didn't really go anywhere for fun.

The more time we had spent trying to be friends, however, the more I started to fall for him. Underneath all that careful control was a man who wanted to let go and enjoy life and I felt special that he allowed me to be a part of that. However, after realizing how badly the Oath could hurt me, Kisten started avoiding me, only interacting with me when he had to, just like he did with everyone else.

It also made sense why Lucius would pair us: as far as he knew, we were still friends and he had always approved of my friendship with Kisten. It sometimes seemed as if he was trying to push us into a relationship, with the way he set up some of our hangouts. He had been surprised when we suddenly stopped and I merely told him that Kisten wanted some space, leaving it at that.

"I don't have much at home," Kisten suddenly spoke, his hands gripping the wheel tightly as his words pulled me from my thoughts. I only continued to watch him in the window's reflection and didn't turn to look at his face. He glanced at me before returning his attention to the road, his tone tentative. "Raiven?"

"I heard you." I sighed, closing my eyes. "You know I don't care. You never have much at home."

"Okay," he stopped talking and returned his attention to driving with my curt answer. We sat in silence for a moment longer before he spoke again, his voice barely above a whisper. "Are you gonna be okay with this?"

"I'm much more worried about you," I admitted, leaning back in my seat as I laid it all the way back. I opened my eyes to stare at the roof of the car, frowning slightly. "You're the one who started avoiding me, remember?"

"It's not like I wanted to. But the Oath..." His voice trailed off as he considered his next words and I sighed heavily, closing my eyes. When he spoke again, his voice was quiet as he took his exit off the highway, leaning back as he stopped at the light. "It's not like I didn't miss you."

"I missed you too," I admitted, my heart aching as the light changed. I paused, opening my eyes to watch the trees fly by the window as we drove closer to his residence. My voice was barely above a whisper when I spoke again, filled with my longing. "Every time I have to see other people being happy together, I miss you."

"At least I wasn't the only one," he laughed slightly, moving his hand to touch my leg. Halfway through the movement, it was almost as if he realized what he was doing and he stopped himself, his hand hovering awkwardly. I looked down as he pulled his hand back to the wheel, clearing his throat. It was another long moment before he spoke, turning into his neighborhood. "I just don't want to hurt you, Raiven."

"Like I said earlier, you never have. That's all the Oath's doing, and well..." I paused as he pulled into his driveway, backing his car into the garage as it opened. "If you want to be technical, we both know whose fault that is."

"Mater Vitae?"

"Her too." I let my seat up and unbuckled myself as he turned off the car. Deep in my mind, I blamed Mother for everything that happened and most Supernaturals did. She created us, bound us all to her with her blood, and then placed us in a world where, until recently, we were hated, feared, and killed. Now, as far as most of us knew, she was hidden, protected by her loyal Hunters.

Fairies were her last creation before most of us denounced her and shortly after, she retreated, although no one knows why or where. I had my own suspicions as to why, but I had no interest in trying to confirm them.

Kisten unlocked his door and bolted inside his house as I took my time noticing the changes he had made to the garage. I hadn't been in his house during the past year and unsurprisingly, there were hardly any changes. Kisten only occasionally updated his home and hadn't moved from this plot of land since he and Lucius arrived back in the 1800s. He had the garage added shortly before I came to Decver, and only did so because of the city complaining about the state of his driveway.

As such, the inside of his house always had an air of nostalgia and I breathed it in as I stepped inside. Kisten was busy closing his curtains and turning on lights, clearly not expecting to have been gone all afternoon. I leaned in the doorway, watching him as he moved about, starting to notice certain changes about him. Kisten's hair was slightly longer than usual, as it was starting to reach his shoulders. He also seemed to have gained a little weight, filling out his shirt a little better than I remembered. While an amazing cook, Kisten only ate enough to stay alive and rarely ate for pleasure, meaning his weight gain was probably muscle.

"Uh, Raiven?" I shook my head as Kisten moved in front of me, a worried look on his face. I looked up to him, slightly embarrassed.

"Huh?"

"I asked if you were hungry." He leaned down close to me, taking in my scent. His eyes shone when he pulled back to look at me again. "You don't smell like you've eaten today."

"You know I don't like it when you do that," I huffed, walking past him to the couch.

Kisten chuckled as he walked into the kitchen, examining what little food he had. He pulled out some ingredients as I switched on his TV, turning to some cartoons. I was barely paying attention, however, my mind returning to Justina as I removed my shoes. I couldn't shake the thought that I knew for certain what could cause wounds like that and the answer was evading me. I closed my eyes as I lay down, seeing Justina's wounded body as I held her in my lap. Large gashes as if ripped open by claws, but somehow all avoiding vital areas. Was Justina attempting to defend herself and that's why they broke her legs?

"Why not just kill her, though?" I wondered out loud, looking up to the roof. Spellcasters weren't difficult to kill: their lifespans were only slightly longer than humans and, besides their use of magic, anything that could kill a human would kill a spellcaster. "To torture her? But why? No one else was—"

"Food's ready." The delicious smell wafted towards me as I sat up, looking toward Kisten in the kitchen. He was portioning food on a plate as I wandered up to him and sat at his breakfast bar. He slid a plate with the appetizing food in front of me: it was some sort of chicken and pasta and one bite confirmed my suspicions. My hunger consumed me and I wolfed down the food with all the vigor of a starving animal. Kisten laughed as he watched, leaning on the counter.

"There's more if you want." He nodded to the

skillet and I paused in my eating, slightly embarrassed by my behavior.

"You aren't going to eat?"

"Not hungry. I hunted yesterday." Kisten tapped his hand on the counter, smiling at me. Kisten's nearest neighbors were miles away and a decent stretch of woods separated them all. Sometimes Kisten would hunt in the woods, helping himself to any prey he could find. He said it helped to keep his animal in check, and he encouraged all the predator shifters to do so, allowing them to come over whenever they wanted to indulge their animal. Sometimes he would go with the newbies to help them, but he often let them figure it out for themselves.

"You're a good Alpha." I commented, smiling as I took my time finishing my food. His smile broadened slightly at that, and he reached for my free hand. I let him take it and winced as he started stroking the back of my hand, feeling the skin burning slightly. Kisten must've noticed as he quickly released me, standing up from the counter.

"I'll be right ba—"

"Don't go," I choked out, trying to swallow my food so I could stop him. He paused in his movement, leaning against the counter on the opposite side of the kitchen. He was looking away from me, not turning to my gaze as I coughed to clear my throat of food. "It didn't hurt that much. Just unexpected. Usually, just touching my hands doesn't hurt."

"Intentions matter." Kisten sighed, running his hand through his hair as he finally turned around. "Whether I want to be intimate matters."

"Want to be..." I let the sentence trail, keeping my eyes on Kisten as I finished eating. He was still refusing to look at me, keeping his eyes to the floor. He had started to unbutton his shirt while cooking and I could see the hair on his chest, lighter in color than the dark brown waves that graced his crown. Kisten looked so majestic in his simple dress clothes, hiding the passion I knew he kept under lock and key. I finished my food, continuing to undress him with my eyes.

"You want to be intimate, huh?" I purred, standing up as I carried my empty plate into the kitchen. I reached around him to drop the dish into the sink, sliding my bandaged hand around his waist.

"Raiven..." Kisten looked at me as if he feared my intentions, and I smiled, wrapping my other arm around him. Kisten seemed torn between returning my gesture and pulling away, before finally settling on lightly touching my shoulders, careful to stay on clothing. I gripped his shirt tighter, pressing myself into him. I earned myself a soft gasp of surprise and I smiled coyly, looking up to his face.

"Yes, Kisten?" I asked, pressing my body more into his as several expressions passed through his beautiful features. As much as I found Kisten's control attractive, I wanted him to let go. I wanted to see the passion he had only let me experience sparingly, just enough to make me want more.

"Raiven don't do this," he pleaded, his hands digging into my shoulders as he fought himself. I smiled, burying my face into his chest. Ignoring his plea. I pressed my leg between his, and I could feel him as he started to become aroused. He was looking for a way to escape me, but his own desire betrayed him as he kept his grip on my shoulders. My own desire began to grow as I slid my hands up his back and dug my fingers into his skin.

He gasped at the movement and without thinking, he grabbed my chin and slid his mouth across mine. My lips and mouth exploded with fire as he kissed me deeply, forcing his tongue into my mouth. Despite the pain, I felt heat growing in another part of my body and I returned the gesture, sliding my tongue against his as the scalding heat consumed my face. It was as if my skin would burst into flames if the kiss continued, but Kisten pulled back, panting heavily. I was also breathing heavily, touching my lips as the heat began to fade.

"Are you alright?"

"Yeah." I smiled, wincing slightly as I dropped my hand back to his waist. Kisten had a dark look on his face, his chartreuse eyes swirling. His devilish expression reminded me more of Crispin, but on him, it only excited me. Kisten moved his hands from my shoulder to my waist, a smirk on his face.

"Good." With this, he kissed me again and I moaned with both pain and desire. It felt as if he were literally setting me on fire with his touch and it excited me as much as it hurt. I could feel his fingers as he fumbled at my shirt and searing pain followed his hand as he touched my back. I merely clung to him as he stroked me, indulging in his own desires.

It was clear his control was fading as Kisten pulled back again, his fangs visible in his mouth as he panted. I took this moment to free myself of him, leaning against the breakfast bar across from him. Kisten made as if he was going to follow me, but gripped the sink behind him, attempting to restrain himself. Both of us were panting as we watched the other, and I smiled, despite the ache left from his touch and his kiss.

"Gods, Kisten, keep this up and you'll make me a masochist." I breathed, my smile broadening. Kisten merely growled in response, and I felt a clench in my lower regions. We had barely been alone together an hour, and this is where we were, panting on opposite sides of his kitchen. Neither of us was sure if the Oath would kill me or just make me wish I were dead, but I had stopped caring about that more than a year ago.

"Raiven, I can smell you." Kisten growled, almost as if he were in pain and I grew worried as I saw fur start to sprout on his arms and quickly recede into his skin. I couldn't fathom that Kisten was losing control of his animal: he was far too experienced to lose control like this. "I can smell how wet you are, and it makes me want you more."

I shifted uncomfortably as he said this, looking away and trying to calm myself down. I hated it when Kisten mentioned my own scents to me: it always made me feel dirty and transparent. Kisten laughed darkly at my attempts to calm down and I turned away from him completely, facing the breakfast bar. This turned out to be a mistake as I soon saw Kisten's hands on the counter next to mine, and he pressed himself into me, now fully aroused and making me aware of it. I didn't try to hide my moan as he ground himself against me, leaning down to breathe in my scent.

"My animal wants you," he growled into my ear, and I couldn't help but shudder against him. He lightly dragged his teeth against my skin, careful to avoid scratching me with his fangs and his spots appeared faintly on his hands, despite the lack of fur.

Smelling my desire, my lust for him was finally sending his animal over the edge, and probably for the first time in a long time, he was losing control. *"I want you."*

"Now who's not being fair, Kisten?" I moaned halfheartedly, doing my best not to push myself against him. Kisten, however, did not care for my restraint and grabbed my hips, thrusting me into the counter. I moaned loudly, dragging my nails against the marble as the shifter behind me repeated his action, loosely grabbing my neck and lifting my head up. He slid his other hand down the front of my body, pressing into my stomach.

"I don't care. I haven't cared for a long time," he whispered darkly into my ear, and even through our clothing, I could feel his arousal throbbing, and it caused me to clench in response. His burning grip on my throat tightened for a moment, and Kisten growled into my skin. "I know you don't, either."

He reached under my shirt again, sliding his free hand up to my breasts. Even through the bra, intense heat danced across my skin as he fondled me and he growled again, kissing my neck as he played with me. His nails began growing into claws and I gave into my moans, not even trying to hide my pleasure from him. This is what I had wanted: for Kisten to give in to me, to give into his desires...

I opened my eyes, having a moment of clarity despite the pain and pleasure. This wasn't Kisten giving in to himself. This was him giving in to his animal and I knew that Kisten would regret it if it went much further. I did my best to hold back my moans and fought to find my voice.

"You're right, I don't," I breathed, trying to do

everything to not focus on his breath on my neck and his member throbbing against my back. "But I also don't want you to regret loving me tomorrow."

Kisten stiffened for a moment, his hands relaxing their grip before he released me altogether. His hands reappeared on the counter and it was clear he was trying to rein in the beast. His hands slowly shifted back to being human, and his spots faded, but remained slightly visible on his skin. His throbbing member against my back betrayed where his desires lay, but he was at least trying to regain control of his lust.

Hesitantly, I leaned back against him and he did his best to hold me gently this time, wrapping his arms around my middle. He took a deep breath and released it shakily, burying his face into my short afro. I considered pulling away from him completely, but instead, I gently touched his arm, before carefully resting my arms on his, my skin burning where we touched.

"You're right. I would regret it if this..." Kisten spoke, his voice still containing a slight growl. "I... wouldn't want my first time with you to be like this, with my animal controlling me."

"I won't say it's not hot though." I laughed softly and he chuckled, the sound vibrating in his chest behind me. "Something different."

"You don't have to tell me that," he postured, nibbling on my ear and causing a slight burning sensation there. He leaned down again, licking my earlobe before whispering into it. "I can still smell how much you want me."

"Kisten," I whined, closing my eyes in embarrassment. He laughed again, pressing kisses into the back of my neck, each one a burning sensation of pleasure and pain.

"You say you hate it, but I love it. I love knowing exactly how much you want me." He spoke in between his kisses, slowly sliding one of his hands under my shirt again. The pain that seared across my middle section almost outweighed the pleasurable sensation, but just knowing that he was touching me, that it was Kisten's hand on my skin, made me love the feeling. "How much the pain isn't bothering you. Should've told me how much you loved it."

"I think someone is turning into a sadist," I teased, reaching my bandaged hand up to stroke his face, my fingers burning as they touched his skin. He removed his hand from under my shirt and I was both disappointed and relieved. Suddenly, I was lifted into the air and I reached to grab Kisten as he lifted me up and walked towards his couch. He turned off the television and climbed on top of me, settling between my legs. I fully expected him to drop on top of me, but he remained on his knees, keeping my legs spread with his hands. I reached up to him, laying my hands on his. "Where was this lack of control a year ago?"

"This is all your fault. All your teasing touches, always wanting me, despite me doing my best to stay away. It was only a matter of time before you would win." His eyes swirled again, and I could still see his fangs as he smiled a toothy smile. He lifted my leg to his shoulder, kissing my thigh through the pants. "I could smell it every time, Raiven and it always took so much to walk away. Even now, it's taking all my control not to just take you."

"You call this restraint?" I pulled my hands back, placing them under my head as Kisten laughed again.

77

He laid another kiss on my pants, squeezing my thigh tightly. He leaned down, letting my leg rest on his shoulder as he slid his hands toward my waist.

"I call it compromise." With this, Kisten leaned over, carefully reaching to undo my pants and release me from them. I couldn't help but tense up slightly, but Kisten lightly kissed my exposed thigh before removing the offensive clothing entirely. "Don't worry, I won't undress you more than this."

Before I could question him, I found my lower half being lifted up and Kisten had his face buried in between my legs, breathing in my scent as his hands were carefully placed on my underwear. I couldn't help but be embarrassed as he breathed me in, and I covered my face as he sighed happily. A long, wet lick told me of his intentions, and I moaned slightly, peeking through my arms to look up at him. He had his eyes closed, licking me through my underwear and enjoying both my taste and scent. I still could experience small flashes of heat despite the clothing separating his tongue from me but these small flashes only added to my pleasure. I moaned freely as Kisten enjoyed his treat, keeping my underwear between us as he indulged himself as much as he dared.

8

I woke up the next morning not sure where I was as sunlight streamed on my face. Something on the bed shifted and I finally recognized the dark brown hair that graced the pillow next to me. I smiled, passing his hair between my fingers and pressing my face into him, my body still aching from the torture it had been submitted to.

"That tickles, Raiven." Kisten mumbled, shifting on the bed as he tried to pull away. I giggled, releasing him as I realized I was wearing a dark red shirt and underwear, different from the blue I had passed out wearing.

"It's not my fault you have beautiful hair," I sat up, looking around for my clothing and my pants. A frown started on my face as I failed to find them, and I shook Kisten gently. "Kisten, what did you do with my clothes?"

"They're in the hamper," he yawned, stretching out like a cat on the bed and his toes curling as the sheet shifted down. He opened his eyes and pointed to the small hamper that was overflowing with dirty clothes. "I didn't want to leave you in soiled clothing, so I managed to find some clothes you had left here. It's getting cold outside, so I tried to choose something warm."

"Okay, but what about my pants?"

Kisten groaned as he motioned towards a chair in the corner, with my pants laid neatly across it. I fell back down, yawning loudly as I tried to finish waking up. Kisten was shirtless but was still wearing pants as he lay next to me, fighting a yawn of his own. I didn't remember him ever taking off his shirt, but from the lingering sensation on my arms, I had a suspicion that he had fallen asleep holding me.

I kissed his hair again as I stood out of the bed, surprised by how refreshed my body seemed. My body felt looser and more limber, despite the ache from the pain. I stretched toward the roof, curling my fingers in the air.

"Do you have anything to do today?" I turned around on hearing Kisten's voice and he was lying on the pillow, watching me as I stretched. I looked away, considering what my next steps would be. I wanted to search for Justina's assaulter, but I still didn't have much information to go on. There wasn't much I could do without visiting the office, but having to take Kisten with me would cause too many questions that I didn't want to have to answer.

"I haven't decided," I admitted, sitting back down on the bed, and Kisten shifted behind me, his arms appearing around my stomach. I hummed happily, stroking his arm despite the pain to my hand. "I'm tempted to go to the Coven to check out Justina's room and see the scene for myself. But I can't exactly take you to the office with me."

"Well, I'm supposed to go visit one of the newbies

who's having trouble shifting and there was a mer-folk who is having issues with her pool and wanted help recalibrating it." He sighed, echoing my hum of contentment. "We could swing by the Coven, then you could join me in helping the pup, and I can drop you off at the hospital while I help the other shifter. I need to check in on Justina and remove your stitches. If you need to go to work, I can drop you off after that."

"So eager to have me break Lucius' order, huh?" I laughed and Kisten chuckled slightly as he squeezed me. "What happened to having to follow orders?"

"You're only as bound as you want to be, remember?" Kisten laughed, echoing the Overseer's words. "But if that sounds good to you, we should leave soon."

"Sounds good." A faint kiss on my back and I felt the bed move as Kisten stood up and moved to his closet to dress. He peeled off his dress pants and changed into a pair of jeans and a plain green t-shirt. I was surprised Kisten owned such clothing as I had never seen him wear anything so normal before. I slowly stood up and slipped on my own pants as Kisten slid on a simple pair of boots. I glanced around for my shoes, remembering I had taken them off next to the couch.

I started out of Kisten's room when a strong hand grabbed my arm and pulled me against him. He was standing in front of his mirror and looking at us to-gether, holding me tightly against him. Kisten's eyes were looking at me lovingly, and he gently buried his face in my neck, sighing happily. I couldn't help but smile at his immature gesture, and I sighed as well, loving the feel of his arms around me. My thoughts turned to the previous night, and I couldn't help the clench in my middle as I remember the torture Kisten had subjected me to. The man in question looked up, his eyes darkening as he caught the change in my scent.

"Here I am being sweet and *someone* is thinking dirty thoughts," he whispered darkly, his eyes still locked with mine through the glass as he grinned. I cleared my throat as my face flushed and freed myself from his embrace. He allowed me to go, his hands lingering as I slid from him.

"Maybe we should leave before we're stuck in this house all day." I mumbled, escaping down the stairs and could hear Kisten's laugh behind me as he followed, his feet heavy on each step. Somehow, hearing his slow steps down the stairs only served to arouse me more and I almost ran into the living room to try to escape my own thoughts.

"You make it sound like you don't want that," his deepening voice followed me down the stairs as I sat on his couch to slide on my boots. Kisten walked into the kitchen, retrieving his keys from the counter as he chuckled to himself over my embarrassment. I stood up to find Kisten standing over me, and he stole a kiss, burning my lips with his indulgence. "Your body says otherwise."

"Don't we have somewhere to be?" I tried to escape him, walking around the couch away from him, but Kisten stopped me, pinning me against the back of the couch. I leaned back as he leaned into me, chuckling. "Kisten, c'mon."

"What? Aren't you the one who started this last night?" He laughed, leaning down and breathing against my neck. There was no sign of his spots or fangs, so this was him acting without the influence of his animal. Kisten's eyes burned and I had to fight the smile that wanted to creep on my face. "Not up for finishing what you started?"

"I thought you did that." I pouted, closing my eyes as he licked my neck. The trail of fire left by his tongue was starting to excite me and I did my best to ignore the heat growing elsewhere in my body.

"I finished what *I* started," he corrected me, taking my hand and pressing it to his groin, allowing me to feel his throbbing member beneath the fabric. I inhaled sharply and I couldn't help but stroke him and earn myself a soft moan. My whole body ached with the thought and desire to have him love me, but I knew the Oath made such a thing impossible. There was a chance we could find a way around it, just as Kisten had the night before, but we also had more important tasks than finding a way around his Oath.

"Let's continue this tonight," I breathed, trying to be a voice of reason in the madness of our passion as I pulled away. Kisten growled in response, and I stroked his cheek, my wrists growing weak from the pain. "Work first, play later. Trust me, I've been wanting this from you for over a year, and I don't want to risk you changing your mind."

Kisten considered my words, closing his eyes and standing away from me. By the time he reopened his eyes, they were back to normal and he smiled softly at me. His grin still held darker things as he turned away from me, jingling his keys in his hand. I followed the Alpha into the garage as he unlocked the doors and I slid quietly into the passenger seat. Kisten also climbed in without making a sound and started up his car, the electric engine practically silent compared to my noisy guzzler.

I watched the scenery fly past us as he drove us back into the city, my thoughts heavy with a new fear as he drove. I had already seen the true extent of Justina's injuries, and I was worried what the scene would look like for her to be injured so badly. My thoughts were in such turmoil that I barely noticed as Kisten pulled into the parking lot behind The Dream and was only brought to the present when the shifter lightly touched my shoulder.

"We're here." He offered and I slowly climbed out of the car, my hand lingering on the door as I looked toward the Coven's entrance. I closed the car door and began to walk to the simple entrance, each footstep heavy as I forced myself forward. I threw the door open, the sound of it banging the wall reminding me of Aurel's anger the day before. I looked past the barrier into the encroaching darkness and I paused, unsure in my movements. Justina was usually the one who maintained the barrier protecting the Coven, so I could only imagine Yoreile was doing it in her place.

"Are you okay, Raiven?" Once again, Kisten's voice drew me from my thoughts and I glanced back towards him. He was leaning against his car, a worried expression on his face and he pushed himself away from the vehicle as he walked towards me. I took a deep breath, turning to face the dark Coven stairs once again.

"I'm fine," I insisted, passing through the barrier and climbing down the dark stairwell as my eyes slowly adjusted. The hallway grew darker as Kisten closed the door behind us and I reached the last step, bypassing the living room on my way to Justina's room. I could see the outlines of Quinn and Yoreile as they stood guard over the scene, both quietly talking amongst themselves. Lucius always took protecting crime scenes very seriously, and I wasn't surprised that he was treating this case no differently.

"It's just me," I announced my presence as I saw Quinn tense, the wraith's red eyes glowing as he summoned his power. Upon recognizing me, he released it, giving me a tired smile. Yoreile remained silent, not turning as Kisten and I approached. "I'm just here to see the scene as an agent, not as a Coven member."

"Go ahead," Yoreile whispered, still barely paying any attention to me as I stood in front of him. I slowly pushed the door open and had to immediately cover my mouth from the display and smell. Her room was barely recognizable: it was as if a hurricane had rampaged through the space and the amount of damage seemed unnecessary to kill a single person. There were various scratches and marks in the walls and overturned furniture, along with several dried splashes of blood and the obvious puddle from where the Overseers had found her sitting.

"If I wasn't sure before, I am now." I muttered, forcing myself to enter her room and examined the damage more closely. Kisten remained in the doorway behind me, keeping his distance as I squatted next to the dried puddle of blood. "This is the same killer."

"What gives it away?"

"The spread of the damage. The blood. It looks just like all the other scenes." I motioned to the destroyed room as I stood. "If anyone else had been in here, they would've been killed. Honestly, from this amount of damage to the room, it's miraculous that Justina survived at all. This attack was violent and fast, and it must've taken all her strength to avoid getting killed..."

My voice faded as I considered what I had said, my eyes looking to the overturned bed where it now sat against the far wall. There was no way a random supernatural did this: it had to be someone who knew who and what Justina was, and had every intention of killing her for it. Justina had a temper and it often came back to bite her, but she never picked undeserved fights or ones she couldn't win.

"Are... are you done, or..." Kisten's voice trailed off as he looked away from the scene, it obviously being too much for him to continue looking at. I looked around the room one more time, taking a couple of photos with my phone and scanning the room to capture the scene.

"Yeah. I'll send the scene recreation to Chris for analysis later." I said, walking back to him in the entryway and resisting the desire to press myself into him.

Yoreile quietly closed the door behind me and I nodded to the warlock. He merely looked away, not saying a word to me but I caught the worried expression on his face. Yoreile was often mistaken for a sorcerer due to the powers he inherited from his ala father, so he understood Justina's struggles well. He wasn't very vocal, but I couldn't help worrying as I stared at his fire red hair. Quinn seemed to sense my thoughts and he was quick to smile at me.

"Don't worry, I won't let anyone get close enough to hurt El here," he quipped, his grey hair falling over his shoulder. He was clearly trying to lighten the mood and I couldn't help my slight smile. "I'm keeping an eye in the darkness, so you two just worry about saving Justina and catching the one who did this."

"I plan to," I agreed, without trying to hide the anger in my voice. Yoreile finally glanced at me, his brown eyes meeting mine before he nodded, turning his gaze back to the wall.

"Let's go. *Der Welpe*[1] is probably suffering." Kisten began walking back towards the surface and I followed him, collapsing into the passenger seat as he started up the car. Kisten placed his hand on my leg this time, carefully backing out and on the road. As we sped away from the Landing, I couldn't help but fall asleep to the steady vibration of the engine.

9

I was running through tall grass, the sounds of screams and vicious growling echoing behind me. My sister's body hung limply against me, unresponsive as I dragged her away from the chaos and carnage behind us. I could hear our fellow tribe members being slaughtered, but I closed my eyes to their plight. All that mattered, all that I cared about, was getting away with my sister. As long as I still had her, everything would be okay.

"Don't worry," I breathed, my panic growing as her blood continued to drip down her body, drenching my simple coverings. I fought my own fear and continued to drag her, refusing to stop. Stopping meant death and I couldn't, wouldn't, let her die. Tears started to stream down my face as I passed through the grass, doing my best to keep moving. "I'll be brave this time, no more running. I won't fail you this time."

I glanced down and the body was no longer my sister's, but Justina's, her dark blue hair matted with fresh blood. I looked back up and found myself in an endless void of darkness, the grasslands disappearing as I paused with Justina's body. The sounds of my tribe dying still echoed in the blackness around me and I glanced around, confused at the sudden darkness.

"Why..." I looked back down as Justina spoke, but it was my sister's voice instead of the sorcerer's. She suddenly jerked her head up, the creature's face a grotesque mismatch of the two women, murderous intent in their eyes. It leapt at me, pinning me down as it tried to strangle me, and I thrashed beneath the creature. My wrist started to burn as I tried to push them off, but they only pushed down on me with more force. The eyes of both my sister and Justina glared at me, burning with hate as they pushed their hands more into my throat. "It should've been YOU!"

"NO!" I screamed, waking from my dream drenched in sweat, Kisten holding my wrist. The wooden locket was also warm against my chest, and I could feel my sister's presence, although she didn't speak.

"Are you alright?" Kisten never took his eyes off the road as he released me, the burning sensation fading. I breathed in deeply, blowing the air out through my mouth as I tried to calm myself. The lingering dreads of the dream still echoed in the back of my mind, and I absently grabbed my sister's locket.

"I'm fine, just... a bad dream," I whispered, stroking the wood that kept my sister with me. Taking her locket and placing her soul inside was the last act I had done for her, and it was a decision that I could never escape from. Assured that I would be fine, I felt her presence leave me and I dropped my hand, sighing heavily.

"It's okay." Kisten reached back over, this time

placing his hand on my legs. I gingerly placed my hand on his and he smiled, never taking his eyes off the road as I weaved my fingers with his. A tingling of pain spread across my skin as I held his hand, but I ignored it, allowing the soft touch and pain to help pull me away from the terrible nightmare.

"We're here." Kisten pulled into a gated community and after giving the name of the resident, drove in. The houses were nice enough, but were much too close together for my liking. I liked to have space in-between me and my neighbors and considering his home, I knew Kisten felt the same way.

After turning down a side street, Kisten pulled into the driveway of one of the many houses, and a middle-aged man ran outside to greet us.

"Thank goodness, Kisten! I'm not sure what happened, but he tried doing it on his own again." The father sounded panicked, and Kisten quickly embraced him, patting his back. The man returned the gesture, the panic and fear plain in his body. Kisten remained calm, pulling away to meet the man's gaze as he spoke.

"It'll be alright, where is he?"

"The backyard." The man huffed and the Alpha quickly nodded. Kisten walked around the outside of the house to a side fence, the father and me following behind. The young boy was in a corner of the yard, trapped in between being human and being a wolf. His legs almost looked broken as they were trying to change into hind legs and his face had already elongated into a snout. His whimpering broke my heart as his fur started to break through his skin and Kisten slowly walked up to him, talking softly.

"It's okay, you can do this. You don't have to be

afraid," he soothed, half-shifting himself to match the boy. He dropped to all fours, crawling next to the frightened teenager. The boy whimpered again, shuffling further into the corner, fur receding back into his body as he tried to turn back to being human.

"I... No! I don't want to hurt anyone!" he cried and I could see the tears pouring from his canine eyes.

I glanced back toward the house and saw a woman and a young girl watching from a porch door. The girl was looking at her brother with concern and even at this distance, I could see the painful look on the mother's face. I looked back to the father and saw tears in his eyes as well.

"Are you..." I asked softly, and the man turned to look at me, at first with confusion but then shaking his head. He looked to the house, locking eyes with his wife for a moment before his expression turned painful.

"No, she's the shifter. I'm human," he tried to smile at her, but it failed to reach his eyes and I looked back to the house, my heart breaking for her. It must've been difficult to watch her son struggle like this, knowing it was her fault her son was suffering, and she could do nothing to help him. The man took a deep breath, trying to steady his voice before continuing. "She's tried to help him, but he gets too scared of the animal taking over. She's never able to get through to him, and it takes all her effort to get him to shift back. We figured with his experience, Kisten could succeed where she failed."

I returned my gaze to Kisten, who was still whispering to the boy, sitting on his hind legs beside him. The teen looked at Kisten, seeing that he was half-shifted as well and Kisten smiled at him. The boy's face filled with concern and he leaned into Kisten, sniffing the air between them. He kept rubbing the boy's back with his furry hand, doing his best to soothe him. "The wolf is a part of you, he won't do anything you don't want. You have complete control."

"It... doesn't hurt?"

"No, if you don't fight it, it doesn't hurt," Kisten soothed, licking the boy's face with his sandpaper tongue. "Your wolf just wants to share your world. He wants you to let him in. Your mother's wolf wants to see her son."

"Her son?" The boy glanced at the house to his mother, who raised her hand to the glass, tears rolling down her cheeks. Kisten nodded, following his gaze.

"Yes, Travis. Just as you have two mothers, she has two sons. A human son, and a wolf son." Kisten hummed. "She wants to share both worlds with you, just like your wolf."

"Mom's... Mom's wolf is hurting too?" Travis looked back to Kisten and it seemed as if the Alpha's words were getting through to him. "But, my wolf doesn't feel like hers."

"Because your wolf is you, and you are your wolf. He's not going to feel like your mother's, but he still won't do anything you wouldn't do yourself." Kisten backed away, getting onto all fours again. "You just have to stop fighting. It'll be okay – I'll be right here beside you."

It was clear his words were reaching the boy and Travis started to calm down. Slowly, the teen got on all fours, matching Kisten, closing his eyes as he lay on the grass. Kisten licked his face again, comforting him and encouraging him to let the transition happen. The boy's hind legs finished shifting, fur beginning to sprout through his clothing as the fabric ripped due to his changing form. Kisten's clothing was made of an expensive material that allowed him to shift without ripping, and he continued whispering and encouraging the young boy, shifting back to being human as the boy's change was complete. The large wolf that replaced him panted, licking Kisten's face while wagging his tail.

"Travis!" The porch door flung open, and the boy's mother ran out of the house, shifting to join her son. The two wolves playfully circled one another, yapping and pawing at each other. The man wiped away his tears and picked up his young daughter as she came over to him, dragging two robes on the ground behind her. The girl looked to where Kisten stood with the wolves, lovingly scratching their ears.

"Is broder okay now?" she asked, looking up to her father as he took the clothing from her. "No more hurt now?"

"Yes, sweet pea." Her father hugged her tightly, his relief obvious in his motions. "I think he's going to be fine now."

Kisten walked over, flanked by his two charges and the mother licked her daughter's face as the father placed the young girl back down. The girl turned to her brother and he backed away for a moment before lowering his head to the ground. She walked up to her brother and patted his head before wrapping her small arms around his neck, hugging him tightly.

"Wolf Broder!" she exclaimed, and he whined happily, his tail thumping the ground behind him. Kisten stood next to me as the whole family embraced, the mother and son shifting back to human.

The father quickly draped the robes over his wife and son and they all turned to face us, bowing their heads to Kisten.

"Thank you so much, Kisten," the woman said, her eyes still shiny with tears as she held her robe tightly. "Thank you for helping my son."

"My pleasure, Rachel." Kisten brushed her off, grasping her shoulders before hugging her tightly. "It's my responsibility as an Alpha and a friend to be there for my pack, no matter how young."

He patted the head of the young boy, who leaned into the touch before leaning against his mother. Kisten's smile was soft and fatherly as he pulled his hand away, meeting the young boy's gaze. "You're not afraid anymore, right?"

"It was... weird. Nothing like I thought it would be," Travis admitted, glancing away as he spoke. Rachel seemed concerned for a moment, but Travis lifted his head as he continued. "But you were right, I was still me. My body was different, but I was me."

"Of course you were," his mother cooed, kissing his forehead as she pulled him against her. "And I'll always be with you, helping you control your wolf."

"Good," Kisten nodded, stepping back to my side as I stood in the yard awkwardly, feeling out of place with the proceedings. I had seen plenty of new animal shifters who had been afraid to shift, but not being one myself, I had never been able to help them. Kisten had probably seen much more of it than me and the expert way he calmed Travis showed his patience and skill. Kisten wrapped his arm around me, nodding to the boy's parents as he pulled me closer. "Well, I have another member of the pack to check on, so we have to excuse ourselves, unfortunately."

Rachel raised her eyebrows at the sight of Kisten's arm around my waist and looked up to my face, sniffing the air in my direction. I cleared my throat, uncomfortable with her scrutiny.

"Is she new to the pack?" she asked, and I couldn't help but cough to hide my embarrassment as I turned away. I hadn't met many of Kisten's pack: in an area as large as The Capital, his pack had hundreds of members and I mostly stayed out of shapeshifter affairs. I always tried to distance myself from becoming too close with anyone who wasn't a part of the Coven, because if they ever committed a crime, I would probably have to be the one to put them down.

Kisten tightened his arm around me, and I looked up to see him smiling broadly.

"Not yet." Before I could refute him, he turned me around and started walking away with me. Once we were back in the front yard out of their sight, he released my waist and turned to look at me, noticing the incredulous look on my face. "What?"

"What do you mean, not yet?"

"Exactly what I said. Not yet." Kisten smiled, his eyes swirling once again. I did my best to look away, but he grabbed my chin, forcing me to meet his gaze. I breathed heavily from the burning sensation on my face, but Kisten didn't release me. Last night seemed to have caused Kisten to throw away most of the restraint he had previously shown, and he only loosened his grip on my chin instead of dropping his hand all together.

"But Kisten, I'm not a shapeshifter, I can't join your pa—"

"As my mate, shapeshifter or not, you're a part of my pack. My Beta." At his mention of the word *mate*, my heart leapt into my throat, and I looked away from him again. Kisten pulled me closer and released my face, pressing my head into his chest. I could hear his heartbeat and couldn't help the shudder that ran through me.

"Kisten, I can't be your mate. You're still bound by the Oath." I spoke into the fabric of his shirt, hugging him tightly. My own chest ached with my words; I didn't want to turn him down, but I knew that there was so much more than what we wanted and other factors that made a relationship complicated. I heard his heartbeat quicken at my mention of the Oath and I hurried my next sentence. "My job also requires that I don't get too close to other Supernaturals and I still have the Hunters to worry about on top of that. I... it's too dangerous for you to be with me."

"You can figure it out with your job. I doubt they'll just drop you after all these years," Kisten stated and I looked up to him, my chin still resting against him. He was looking down at me, his expression showing how serious he was. "As far as the Hunters are concerned, having you as my Beta puts me in no more danger than being Lucius' Alpha. And the Oath and Evalyn... I'll deal with that when the time comes."

"But Kis—"

"I have tried to restrain myself for far too long and abide by rules that don't serve me or my desires. I have only cared for two people in my long life, and last night reminded me how lonely I've allowed myself to become. I can't... No. I refuse," Kisten paused, leaning down to kiss me deeply, once again setting my mouth ablaze. He gripped me tightly, his longing and desperation evident in his touch and kiss. I was left panting when he released me, my body growing weak in his arms. His voice was soft as he spoke again, lovingly stroking my face. *"I refuse to lose you."*

With this, Kisten released me and continued walking to his car, leaving me in a daze behind him. Court me, make me his Beta... he had basically done the human equivalent of asking me to marry him. I wanted nothing more than to say yes to him, but there were so many obstacles to that sort of future that he seemed to be overlooking.

No, not overlooking, I thought to myself as I followed him into the car, unable to help the warmth in my chest from his words. *Just determined to overcome.*

As we pulled out of the neighborhood and began to head to the hospital, I couldn't help but smile at the thought of Kisten belonging to me.

10

Kisten left me in the waiting room as he walked back to his car, telling me he should be back shortly. As soon as he left, I felt the sting from disobeying Lucius' order but I shrugged it off, quickly making my way to the Supernatural wing. I stood outside Justina's door, closing my eyes as I prepared myself to see my friend. My mind kept flashing to my nightmare and my sister's body, but I shook my head to clear it of those images as I stepped inside.

LeAlexende sat on the opposite side of her bed, dead or asleep in the chair. It was a little after two, so I knew he would overpower death's hold on him soon and I stepped up to Justina's bed, closing the door softly. She was still unconscious, but her breathing was steady, as if she were merely sleeping. I noticed the many bandages on her arms and midsection, as well as both of her legs in casts. I noticed her left arm was also in a cast, and I gently touched her right hand. She didn't move in response, and I squeezed her fingers, fighting to hold back my tears.

"Wake up soon, Justina." I whispered, moving

some strands of blue hair as I kissed her forehead. "Help me punish the one who did this to you, *cecmpa*[1]."

The door opened behind me and I moved to the opposite side of the bed near LeAlexende, allowing the nurse to enter. They simply went to work, checking her vitals and running simple checks, ignoring my presence. The nurse was a witch, as I recognized him as one Justina sometimes got drinks with when she went out. He seemed distressed at having to see her like this, but he acted with full professionalism as he worked. Soon, the nurse left with the blood samples to take to the lab, and I remained, looking at the sleeping spellcaster.

I sighed heavily, looking to LeAlexende as the Overseer awoke, flooding the room with power as he escaped Death's grasp. It always felt so dramatic when an elder vampire awoke: the room flooded with energy, a wave of power as they pulled themselves back from the grave. He looked first to me, beaming a soft smile before picking up his phone.

"Have you been here long?" he asked and I shook my head as he checked his missed messages, barely acknowledging my answer. "Good, good, I woke up on time."

I remained silent as I leaned against the wall, unsure of what to do or say. After sending a reply to one of his messages, LeAlexende turned to face me, smiling his cheery smile.

"Kisten's not with you?" he inquired, and I shook my head, unable to resist smiling slightly. LeAlexende hummed thoughtfully, looking at his phone as it vibrated in his hand again. "I'm sure he'll be by later to check on her then. He's become a good doctor."

"He has. He really cares for everyone," I breathed, looking towards the door. My thoughts turned to Evalyn and I shook my head, my smile fading. The Overseer gave me a strange look as I frowned, his blond hair shifting slightly. "Almost everyone."

"Ah, you are referring to Luc's new Retainer?" I gave LeAlexende a strange look, as I had never heard anyone dare call Lucius Luc, not even Eve. I guess being an old friend and an Overseer gave him the right, or at least made him feel comfortable enough to do so. The vampire's smile faded slightly as I nodded and he turned his eyes to the floor. "I must admit, I am not very fond of her, either."

"Really no one is." I shrugged, looking away to a corner again. Something about meeting LeAlexende's gaze was uncomfortable to me, but I couldn't seem to place why. "She doesn't do much to try to change that, though."

"Well, she really does seem preoccupied with her own ambitions." I was surprised how well LeAlexende had been able to read Evalyn despite meeting her for the first time a few days ago. "But Lucius has always had varied tastes and she's not his first ala Retainer. She just seems... a bit more ambitious than the ones he has chosen in the past."

"How long have you known Lucius?" I queried, my curiosity getting the better of me. The caramel vampire ignored me at first, still engrossed with his phone screen. LeAlexende's smile widened as he looked back up to me, and he was genuinely amused.

"Since he was turned. Like him, I'm one of the First and a former member of her court." I looked at him with shock and stepped back a little. My reaction only seemed to amuse him more, although I saw a hint of pain at my discomfort. "Unlike Luc, I changed my identity after I left Mater Vitae. I have no desire to be reminded of my past."

"I..."

He interrupted me, not giving me the chance to speak. "I also know you have changed your name since your time with her, leaving your previous past behind. I'm sure you understand not wanting that burden."

His eyes bore into mine despite his warm smile and I could almost feel his pain. I nodded solemnly, grabbing my sister's locket again through my shirt; those who did not have immortality or long lives failed to understand the burden a name could carry. Just that single word could wound you worse than any weapon and bury you in the sins and grief of the past. My sister rose at my touch and LeAlexende's gaze drifted to my hand.

"Ah, so you still wear it." I looked at him surprised, quickly dropping my hand. LeAlexende laughed slightly, checking his phone again. "Lucius is polite enough to pretend he doesn't remember when you were the Immortal and I doubt he's told your true origins to anyone else but me. To be fair, it's not as if we really knew you, anyway, with the distance she kept you from everyone."

"No one was given the chance," I commented, and my sister drifted away again without saying anything. I knew she was probably still watching me, waiting until I was alone to voice her thoughts. "To Mother, I was a precious pet, only to be appreciated for the rarity I was. I am incredibly grateful to Lucius for his protection and the risk he is taking with me."

"Yes, he is taking a great risk, agreeing to have you

in his Coven, especially being a First himself," LeAlexende agreed and he checked his phone as it vibrated
for what felt like the hundredth time since I entered
the room. "But he always was one to do so. Adds thrill
to such a long life."

"What about you?" I asked, and the Overseer
laughed slightly, answering his message before
looking back up to me.

"Oh no, not me. Just like with changing my
name, I prefer to live free of regrets or burdens."
LeAlexende smiled his relaxing smile and once again,
I couldn't help but return it. "I enjoy my simple life
as an Overseer, providing protection and safety for
my charges as best I can. Hunters aren't much of a
problem for me anymore, and my Retainer is very
capable."

"Is that why you pretended not to recognize me?"
I pushed, and the vampire nodded, looking to the
ceiling before closing his eyes. I realized how little I
knew about the First Thirteen: all I truly knew about
them was their names. I had seen some of them at
times, but there was only one I knew by appearance.
It was no wonder that I had approached Lucius
without realizing who he was and how meeting
LeAlexende had not stirred any memories. My voice
was soft as I spoke again, my mind drifting to the
First who had helped me escape. "Thank you for
helping me, LeAlexende."

"Please, call me Alex. Speaking of helping..." He
opened his eyes, glancing at his phone before returning his full attention to me. "I can tell you confi-
dently that there were no empousa present at any of
your crimes, before or after. All the locations are far
from any Overseers protecting one and none were

traveling through those areas at the time of the murders."

I frowned at this news, not trying to hide my displeasure. The Overseer seemed to view this as good news, as he beamed at me while I spoke. "So, we are looking for a harpy or cyclops with an unknown motive."

"I don't think that's it, either," LeAlexende added, and I looked at him, confused. The vampire shrugged as he looked back to his phone, scrolling through a gallery. "I had my contacts tell me a little about the crimes and neither harpies nor cyclops can kill that many people that fast, or sneak into sealed locations without being seen, ability to pass barriers aside. I think you're looking for a hybrid, someone who has a parent who can overpower magic, but still be able to kill large groups of people."

I considered LeAlexende's words as he spoke. He was right: the last crime had a body-count of more than fifteen, and that was a lot for either of those species to try to kill in the time-frame. It also would've been impossible for either species to hurt Justina as badly as she had been and whoever did it had managed to sneak into the Coven while Crispin and I were out.

"I'll let my team know. Thank you... Alex."

The Overseer nodded, turning his gaze to the door as Kisten finally entered. Kisten was looking down at his screen, nodding as he swiped the information onto the screen next to Justina's bed.

"Blood work looks normal. It seems she's healing herself well, which was my biggest concern, considering how old Justina is." Kisten sighed, the relief obvious on his face and I couldn't help my own relief.

Justina was only in her thirties, but sorcerers rarely lived to fifty, due to their magic eating away at their life. Other spellcasters said it was the price they paid for breaking the laws of magic and so far, no way had been discovered to help them. "I should be able to remove her casts tomorrow and depending on how things go tonight, she may wake up tomorrow."

"Good. I want to catch the one who did this before then, but..." My mind turned to what Alex had said, and I couldn't help my frown. "Honestly, I don't think we will without her help."

"I know. Before we go, I was asked to help with another patient before we leave, so I'll be a moment longer." Kisten smiled at me, a gesture I returned as I turned to him. It wasn't surprising that Kisten had been asked to help, as he often got called in on his days off due to his age and expertise. "But first, come here."

Kisten motioned me to his side and I walked around the bed to meet him. He placed down his tablet before gently taking my bandaged hand and began to remove the gauze he had wrapped it with the day before. My hand was already mostly healed from the wound he had given me and he nodded, pleased with the results. He leaned to retrieve a small pair of scissors and cut the stitches, kissing my hand before releasing me.

"You're good. Go help them," I whispered, waving him away. "I'm fine here."

"Okay." His gaze lingered on me as he turned to walk away, and I was once again left alone with the Overseer. LeAlexende chuckled to himself, placing his phone back down as soon as the shifter left.

"Looking to finally settle down?" he asked innocently, and my face grew warm with a blush as I stammered to answer. He stopped me with a wave of his hand, laughing at my embarrassment. "Kisten just didn't seem the type. He always seemed to be inside his own thoughts."

"We're not together," I managed, my heart pounding in my throat. LeAlexende gave me a look that clearly said he didn't believe me and I hurried my next statement. "He's still bound to Lucius and Evalyn by the Oath and—"

"Ah, he should fix that soon," was all the Overseer offered, picking up his phone again to scroll through something, clearly not bothered by this information. "I would hate to see you two kept from each other over something so trivial."

"If only it was that easy. Eve absolutely hates both of us and she would never agree to release Kisten, to spite us." At this, LeAlexende sighed, setting his phone on his lap. I looked away, wondering if I had said too much but I realized that it felt amazing to get this off my chest. "There are... other factors too. We had been keeping our distance to limit the temptation, but being forced to be together is..."

"Guess all that control isn't for show," LeAlexende giggled and once again, my face flushed with embarrassment. His purple eyes turned serious and I cleared my throat under his scrutiny, once again unable to look at him. His voice was soft and serious as he continued. "The Oath will do its best to kill you if you take it too far."

"Yeah." I nodded, clearly remembering the pain from the night before. LeAlexende looked curiously at my face before returning to being absorbed in his phone. When he spoke again, it made me jump and I barely noticed as Kisten returned.

"I would still say something to Luc. He has known Kisten for a long time and could easily force Eve to release her part. Both of you could use a little happiness in your lives." He offered nonchalantly and Kisten smiled, walking over to me.

"I will, but not yet," he pulled me close again, laying my head on his chest. I couldn't see his or LeAlexende's face as he spoke, and I instead breathed him in. "There are other things that need to be taken care of before I go to Lucius about the Oath."

"A stickler for tradition, I see. Just don't leave any marks on her," Kisten's chest vibrated as he laughed at the Overseer's words and the shifter hugged me tighter. "I'd hate to see you scar such a beauty."

"No promises on that, but I'll take good care of her."

"See that you do." LeAlexende smiled at both of us brightly and settled into his chair. With this, Kisten released me and, still holding my hand, led me out of the room. He didn't say a word as we walked through the waiting room, but I recognized something in his gait was off.

I opened my mouth to ask him as we stepped on the elevator, but Kisten swung me into the wall, quickly pressing the button for the lobby before pressing his body into me. The burning sensation on my wrists as he pinned me to the wall told me clearly where his intentions were and I struggled to free myself. Kisten put a stop to this by kissing me, burning my lips and tongue once more. There was no sandpaper texture to his tongue, so just like this morning, his animal was not behind this assault.

"Can you even begin to understand," he released me from the kiss, interrogating me as he nibbled on my neck. I tried to strain away from him, but he held me firmly in place, the pain radiating from my wrists to my hands and arms. He growled against my skin, the sound beginning to excite me. He noticed the change, as he shoved his knee between my legs, kissing me deeply again. I closed my eyes as I melted under his torture. "How much I missed you? Barely an hour apart, and I felt like I was losing my mind."

"I can tell." I moaned, the intense pain overwhelming my senses. Kisten released me just as we reached the lobby and I nearly collapsed to the floor as the elevator stopped. He stood me up as the doors opened and he led me through the lobby, holding my hand tightly. I knew he wasn't done with me when we reached his car and instead of releasing me, he opened the door to the back and tossed me onto the seat. Kisten climbed on top of me and closed the door, pinning me again.

"What have you done to me, Raiven?" He growled again, and I saw that his fangs had yet to appear. There was no sign of Kisten's animal and knowing this was all him was just as exciting as it was terrifying. He kissed me deeply again, undoing the front of my pants as best as he could in the tight space. I moaned loudly into his kiss as he slid his hand to touch me, the heat almost too much to bear. The underwear Kisten had found for me was much thinner than the pair I had originally been wearing, and I could feel the more intense heat that the previous pair had protected me from. "I've never felt like this. I feel..."

"Unhinged? Free?"

"*Insane.*" He pulled up from me and grinned, licking my face and dragging his tongue down to my neck. The searing fire that followed his tongue caused me to moan again and he pressed his hand into me more, forcing me to try to squirm away from him and his painful touch. However, Kisten already had me pinned to the door and I had nowhere to go as he pushed my underwear to the side, and easily slid his fingers inside me.

I cried out at the first wave of pain as it washed over me, and Kisten silenced me with a kiss, drinking in my pain as he moved his fingers inside me. The pain was overwhelming, and I felt as if I would pass out, but I also couldn't deny the pleasure of having him touch me. Feeling him flex and move his fingers deep inside me made me whimper at the intense pain and pleasure, and I couldn't help it as I squirmed beneath him.

After what seemed like eternity, he finally released me, sliding his fingers from me and pulling back from his kiss. I gasped for precious air as the pain stopped and I ached from the echoes of the heat. Kisten raised his hand to his face, playing with my juices on his fingers before placing them in his mouth, closing his eyes as he indulged in my taste. I felt a clench inside my midsection and, despite the pain it had caused, I couldn't help but want his fingers back inside me.

"You are really enjoying this." He laughed darkly, gazing deep into my eyes as he removed his fingers from his mouth and I merely panted in response, still unable to speak. His gaze softened for a moment and he carefully leaned over me, sniffing my skin. "How hurt are you?"

"I'll live," I murmured, getting my breath under control as I smiled. "I'd love a warm bath to get rid of this ache, though."

"I'll start one as soon as we get home." Kisten smiled at me and I laughed, reaching to touch his face.

"It is interesting to see a different side of you. A passionate side." I admitted and he chuckled, leaning away from me. He almost seemed worried as he gazed at the foggy window, and I didn't like the look that entered his expression.

"You're seeing a repressed side." He sighed, running his clean hand through his hair. "Something about yesterday really did something to me. Whenever I'm around you, I feel like I'm losing all the careful control that I've built up over the centuries."

"It's good to just let go every once in a while." I smiled, settling into a more comfortable position on the seat. Kisten leaned over me, sliding his hand up my shirt as he kissed my neck, once again setting my body on fire with pain. I was beginning to grow used to the heat and it was starting to be less painful and more pleasurable each time I was subjected to it.

He really is making me a masochist, I thought to myself as I strained my neck to give him better access. He used his free hand to slide my hand down to his erection and I squeezed him through the fabric of his jeans. He moaned into my skin, and my body grew more excited with his sounds.

"Even if all I want to do is bury myself inside you, consequences be damned?" He moaned, his voice strained as he spoke. I carefully undid his jeans and slid my hand inside, stroking him through the fabric as I had earlier. His underwear was already wet from

his excitement and I gulped, holding in my own desire as I stroked him, teasing him with my fingertips.

"I won't tell you no." I moaned, not even attempting to hide my desire for him. Every part of my
body wanted him and my heart ached to have him as
he lay on top of me, engrossed in my skin as I played
with him. Kisten purred low in his throat and for a
moment, I wondered if he really was going to take me
in the back of his car. Granted, I'd had sex in worse
places.

"Just makes me want you more," he finally whispered, moving from on top of me as he shifted my
legs until they lay across his lap. He took a deep
breath and let it out shakily, clearly trying to calm
himself down. He patted my legs as he closed his
eyes, focusing on steadying his breathing. "Let me get
us home so we can clean up and I can get you that
bath before we do something I'll regret."

"Sounds great." I closed my eyes as he redid his
jeans and climbed out of the car. I settled in the back
seat as he re-entered on the driver's side and started
it up, driving us back home.

II

I lounged in the warm water, gently blowing on the bubbles that surrounded me. As soon as we had gotten home, Kisten had drawn my bath, taking a moment to use his shower while the tub filled up. I had fallen asleep on the drive back to his house and awoke as he finished undressing me. Kisten said nothing, merely picking me up to place me in the warm water and kissing me before leaving again.

Kisten was taking a moment to go by my house while I bathed, breaking Lucius' order yet again, but I merely shrugged off the annoying sting. Anyone else in the Coven would have been incapacitated by disobeying an order from Lucius, but at worst for me, the stinging would intensify to a mild burning sensation. I was only bound to his orders if I wanted to be, despite taking the Oath of the Coven like everyone else.

Beyond that, I wasn't worried about Kisten: the culprit really had only been interested in Justina. Otherwise, there would've been plenty of other opportunities to attack any of us and if he really was going after sorcerers, Yoreile would be his next choice. A frown started on my face as my thoughts changed to the case and I shifted in the bath.

"Sis." I felt her consciousness rise as I called out to her and I settled further down into my bubbles. She sat quietly as she had done all day, still not speaking to me and I blew into the bubbles again. "What's on your mind?"

'... About what?'

"Anything. Everything. The case." I closed my eyes, sighing as I thought of the man who had been by my side for the greater part of the day. "Kisten."

'Hmph,' she grunted, and I could hear a lecture in her voice. I winced involuntarily: lectures from my sister had never been pleasant, even when she was alive. When I had been alone at Mater Vitae's court, all she ever did was lecture me. About how I should've been using my power to escape, how I shouldn't have bound her to a locket, how much she... hated me for being chosen to live. My guilt began to rise again as flashes of my nightmare flicked through my mind, and I knew she felt it, as her voice was soft when she spoke again.

'Well, this whole Beta thing sounds like your problem. I have no say in that, although we both know what you want.' She sighed, and I could envision her leaning back in a chair, crossing her legs. I smiled slightly and I could hear the smile in her voice as she continued. 'Kisten is probably one of my favorites. You two are nice compliments to one another; he keeps you grounded while you allow him to let go sometimes.'

"I thought you liked Rurubelle." I giggled, remembering a previous girlfriend of mine. I could almost feel my sister's embarrassment as she grunted. "You said she was good for me and I was a fool to give her up."

'*Well, I wouldn't have.*' She pouted, and I laughed out loud, lifting some more bubbles in my hand to blow on. '*But, again, I'm stuck in a locket. I can't have anyone.*'

"I'm sorry." I dropped my head again, the nightmare ever-present in my mind. My guilt over my sister's death was one I could never escape from, as a constant reminder hung around my neck; that, for some reason, I had been chosen to live, while she had died. "I want to fix it, but we already–"

'*Stop it, Raiven. I've told you before, I have already moved past this. Your guilt will eat you alive if you let it.*' She sighed, clearly upset over my reaction to her joke. I stayed silent, fighting tears that wanted to flow as she continued, '*You did what you could at the time. I may have hated you for it originally, but I have had more than enough time to get over it.*'

"I couldn't be without you. I just–"

'*I know, but at some point, you're going to have to let me go. I know you have always been... more dependent than me, but I won't last forever.*' She stated, and I knew she was right. Despite still being alive in some capacity, I knew she was fading. She slept more often than ever before, and now neither of us could remember what her name was. Little by little, her soul was slipping away and even if I could find a way to give her a body again, she probably didn't have enough of her soul left to keep it alive. I could give her peace by returning her to where she was buried, but I wasn't ready to give her up.

From what I remembered of my human life, my

sister was always the more independent and braver one. We had lost our parents young, although neither of us remembered how or why, and the other tribe members had accepted us, but never raised us. It always felt that they knew we were different somehow, even if they didn't know or understand why. It was almost a revered fear that made them keep us around, and less that they wanted anything to do with us. My sister raised me, tried to help me be brave, but my fear of dying and danger always made me run. Even when I was trying to save her life, all I could do was run.

'*As far as your case is concerned,*' my sister spoke again, dragging me from my memories with her voice; she seemed to understand that I was sinking into the past and was trying to bring me back to the present. '*You're still making it too complicated.*'

"Too complicated?"

'*Yes.*' She groaned, frustrated with me for not seeing it from her perspective. '*You're so sure there's a glorified reason your culprit is killing and you're trying to tie the victims together in a way they don't belong. Since we know it's not an empousa, the motive becomes obvious if you look at it from the mind of a simpleton. Justina's attack proves that.*'

"Why else would you..." My voice trailed off as I realized what she was saying. "No unified reason, but simple, individual ones? Simple, petty..."

'*Not everyone will overlook a slight.*' She reminded me and I jumped out of the tub, wrapping the towel around me as I hurried into the bedroom. I snatched my phone off the bed, quickly plugging in Liel's number and waited impatiently for her to answer. My sister remained for a moment, but then faded back to sleep, humming her delight at my understanding. I finally heard Liel's soft, raspy voice on the other end, and she sounded distracted.

"What is it, Raiven? Do you need Crispin?" She sounded as if she was having difficulty keeping her voice down and I wondered if it was time for her to scream again. Banshees had to scream every once in a while to keep their power under control, just like animal shifters shifted to keep their animal in check.

"No, Liel. I just need to know if you and Justina have gone to The Dream within the last week or so." I impatiently tapped my fingers on the sheets as Kisten walked into the room and I saw his confusion. I motioned for him to sit as Liel hummed with thought and he sat on the bed next to me, waiting patiently for me to finish.

"No, I haven't gone with her lately. Haven't really been in the mood." I heard a male voice in the background and assumed it was Crispin as they spoke. He almost sounded out of breath, as if he had come back from exercising. "Actually, Cris says he and her go every Thursday. That's rude. Invite me sometime."

Crispin must've said something else rude because I heard Liel hit him. He laughed in his usual annoying way and I merely sighed on my end.

"Did they meet anyone, anyone Justina could've upset or made angry?" I waited as Liel repeated my question and my anxiety grew as I heard nothing on the other end. I could hear slight whispering before Liel addressed my question.

"Cris says no, but he wasn't there the whole time. She got upset with him over something and he left early. He said she stayed at least another hour by herself before she left."

Without saying more, I thanked Liel and hung up,

immediately dialing Lucius. Kisten opened his mouth to speak but I stopped him with a hand wave, returning my attention to my phone.

"Hello?"

"Lucius." I spoke quickly, determined to follow the path of logic my sister had put me on. "I need the surveillance of The Dream from Thursday night into Friday."

"Done." Lucius said and I think he could tell from my tone that it was related to Justina. I could hear him standing up from his seat, and quickly walking down a hallway. "I'll go get the tapes now, Crispin and Liel will bring them."

"Thank you." I hung up again and this time Kisten spoke before I could stop him. He had moved closer to me on the bed and seemed as if he had something to say.

"Raiven, wait a mome–"

"Not yet." I hand-waved him again as I dialed my boss's number and waited impatiently for it to ring. When he answered, I heard the busy sounds of a restaurant in the background and remembered it was Sunday. Brandon must've taken my warning seriously and went to dinner with Arkrian.

"What's up, Raiven? What can I do you for?" He sounded pleased and I smiled slightly, glad that he had finally taken the initiative. His love for his children was real and I was happy he had put his prejudices aside, at least for one evening.

"I hate to interrupt you when you sound like you're having a good time, but–"

"You were right, this lad isn't half bad." Brandon interrupted me and I huffed, upset that he didn't let me speak. "Did you know that he has a background in football? Even played in college. I thought animal shifters avoided spo—"

"Yes, I am aware." I snapped exasperatedly, my annoyance growing. "But I didn't call to talk about Arkrian. I have a new idea about the case."

"What is it?" All the joy in his voice faded, replaced with the seriousness I was used to. I spoke quickly, standing up from the bed and pacing.

"I think we're looking at the case all wrong. The killings aren't connected in the way we were thinking," I stressed, motioning to Kisten, who handed me the fresh clothes he had bought me from my house, his annoyance on his face. I entreated him with my expression as I continued speaking to my boss. "Can you have Julia and Chris gather all the surveillance they can from any night clubs, bars or similar locations any of our victims may have visited?"

"What are you thinking?" He was intrigued by my suggestion and I paused as I began to dress, carefully placing my phone on the bed as I switched to speaker mode. "We've already pored over hundreds of hours of footage and found nothing."

"That he's a revenge killer." Kisten's expression changed as I said this, and I saw something dark flash across his face. "I think he's killing people who have slighted him or offended him in some way. He's going after a specific person and everyone else is collateral damage. He knows he can kill them, so he just does. It's not about numbers, or killing certain species or anything. Just that person, and anyone else unfortunate enough to be there."

"Fuck, you're on to something." I heard Brandon as he waved down their server and asked for the check. I heard as he apologized to Arkrian before giving me his full attention. "That makes so much sense, it's stupid. It explains the randomness of the killings, why they're so spread out. Why the number of deaths have been on a steady increase and why Justina was targeted alone. Dammit, that's so fucking simple."

"Yeah, he was careful about where he killed before because he didn't know how many he could get away with. Now he doesn't care, being so bold as to even attack Justina at the Coven. He kills the person who slighted him and then," I paused a moment as I pulled the sweater Kisten had bought me over my head. "He leaves to avoid getting caught."

"I'll call Julia and head to the office with her. I'll get Chris to start reaching out to the other Overseers to get us the additional footage." I heard the rush of wind as he stepped out into the evening and hailed the valet. "See if you can find out where Justina has been in the past week. She's our best chance of getting a description of who we're looking for."

"Already working on it." I heard the knock on Kisten's front door downstairs, and he looked at me as I motioned for him to go answer it. His eyes narrowed as he walked away, and I couldn't help but be confused by his reaction as I returned my attention to my phone. "I need to go so I can check the tape. I'll be to the office as soon as I can."

"Keep me updated."

A click on his end and I slid the phone into my pocket, walking downstairs to find Kisten, Crispin and Liel all in the kitchen. As I came down, Crispin held up the flash drive containing the surveillance and I hurried down the last few steps.

"Lucius said this might be related to your case

and what happened to Justina," Liel whispered, keeping her voice low. The banshee was wearing her usual garb – a long, black cloak that hid her form and her white dreads flowing from underneath the hood. Her dark gray eyes matched perfectly with her nearly black skin, and she tugged on her hood nervously. She looked to the flash drive and then back to me, her expression gloomy.

Crispin handed the drive to Kisten, giving him a nod as he did so. Kisten took the drive and walked back up the stairs, speaking quietly.

"Laptop's in the office." I watched him leave and then returned my attention to Crispin, taking in the vampire. With him here, I couldn't help but still wonder what he had wanted to say to me in the garden before we were interrupted. He was looking at Liel, but on noticing me looking, turned to face me. His expression was serious, none of his cockiness or playboy attitude.

"How is she?" He whispered, and I realized that he probably hadn't seen her since Lucius and LeAlexende had carried her away. Liel also looked worried about Justina's state, so it was obvious Lucius hadn't told anyone about her progress. I took a deep breath, meeting their gaze.

"She's hurt, but alright. Kisten says she's healing herself subconsciously and he'll be able to remove her casts tomorrow." Both were relieved at my words, and I heard Kisten coming back down the stairs as I continued. "Hopefully, she'll wake up soon but I'm hoping the footage will help us find the one who did this before that."

Kisten set the laptop on the counter and we all hovered around him as he plugged in the drive and opened the file. The footage began at midnight Thursday morning and Kisten began to scroll through the video.

"We arrived around ten," Crispin offered, watching the time stamp in the corner. "I don't know what time it was when I left, but probably after midnight."

"Stop it when they get there." I insisted, and Kisten obliged, stopping the video after Justina and Crispin walked into frame. They sat at the bar together and ordered their drinks, with Crispin immediately turning to flirt with a girl next to him. Liel and I rolled our eyes at the same time, both turning to look at Crispin in unison. The vampire in question merely shrugged, not bothered by our looks.

"Double the speed," I ordered and once again Kisten obeyed, and we watched with anticipation. The night was normal enough; the dance floor was packed, and people came and went from the bar. Justina remained at the bar all night, drinking her drinks as Crispin flitted back and forth. Then Crispin approached Justina, laying a hand on her shoulder, which she angrily shoved off. "There, slow it down,"

We all watched in silence as Justina angrily gestured at Crispin, clearly done with his constant back and forth. Crispin appeared to be trying to defend himself, but Justina sat back down, ignoring him as she ordered another drink. He tried to talk to her for a little longer before he gave up and left, heading back for the Coven. Shortly after her blowout with Crispin, Justina finished her drink and stood to leave as well, but was stopped by someone.

It looked to be a woman and Justina was clearly excited to see her, embracing her guest tightly and giving her a kiss. The woman was tall, with skin slightly lighter than mine and she was attractive, showing off her toned legs with her short dress and heels. They sat down at the bar together and I reached around Kisten to pause it.

"Do any of you know her?" All three of my companions shook their heads as I took a screenshot and resumed the video.

Shortly after the women sat down, they were approached by another party, a man who was wearing dark clothing. He had his back to the camera, so we couldn't see his face as he talked to the women. Everything was fine at first, with him even buying the girls more drinks. However, he must've said something Justina didn't like because she seemed to excuse herself from the situation. The man was trying to stop her, but Justina was making it clear she was no longer interested in being around him. Her friend was also trying to convince Justina to stay, motioning for her to sit back down, but Justina was having none of it. She brushed her way past the man, and he reached to grab her. Crispin hissed as we watched, all of us knowing what was going to happen.

The man was immediately blown back into the bar, finding himself in Justina's previous seat as she turned to glare at him. The man was still facing away from the camera and moved to turn around. I held my breath, my hand hovering to pause the video as we waited to see his face. The bartender stopped him, however, making it evident that it would be a very bad idea to pursue Justina, who was now leaving the bar using the front door. Her friend was trying to get the man's attention, but he stomped off, leaving the same way Justina had. She sighed, finishing her drink and paying before walking out. As she turned, I paused the video again, got the best angle of her face that I could, and took another screenshot.

"Send those to me," I demanded, leaning away from the laptop and Kisten obeyed, sending the files to my phone. I accepted the images, nodding to myself. "If we can find that man, we find the one who hurt Justina. That woman and the bartender were the only ones besides Justina who saw his face."

"The bartender's Josh," Crispin added, looking at Liel, but the banshee shot him an angry glance. It was clear she blamed him for leaving Justina by herself, but for once, I found myself on Crispin's side. Justina was nothing if not stubborn and she had decided she was done with him for the night. If he hadn't left of his own accord, she would've made him. "But he went out of town Friday to see his mother for the holiday."

"Well, his trip will have to be interrupted for a bit," I spoke bluntly, turning to look back to Kisten's computer. "I'll have him brought into the Local division closest to him so they can question him.

"Meanwhile, I need to get these stills and this video to my team." I ejected the flash drive from Kisten's laptop and started to walk around the breakfast bar when Crispin caught my arm. I whipped around to glare at him, almost instantly summoning my power. "Let me go."

"Wait a moment. I—"

"No." I stopped him, pulling my arm from his grip. Kisten also turned to face Crispin, his face dark. Crispin ignored this and shared another glance with Liel, who turned away, not offering him any assistance. I narrowed my eyes at the pair; this was too similar to how Justina had been with Crispin. "What is it?"

"I have to... tell you something. Just you." His demeanor from the garden returned and my suspicion and confusion increased. I crossed my arms across my chest and interrupted Kisten, who started to stand.

"And it has to be now? I want to find who did this to Justina." I argued and Crispin looked away again, this time looking to the floor. "The longer I hold off on this, the greater the chance that this guy moves again and we lose him."

"I know, and I want to catch him too." Crispin curled his hands into fists and then released them, visibly trying to calm himself down. "I want to do more than catch him. But I have to tell you before she wakes up."

I eyed Crispin, trying to guess his motives. It didn't seem like this was something he wanted to do. Unlike the previous day, where he had played his games before attempting to tell me, he now seemed as if he was being forced. I glanced at Liel, who only met my gaze for a moment before looking away again. She clearly was in on what this was all about, and why Crispin had to tell me before Justina woke up, but the banshee was keeping her distance. I returned my gaze to Crispin, who shuffled uncomfortably.

"And it has to be now?"

"Yes. Please." He replied curtly.

I placed the flash drive back on the counter and motioned Crispin to follow me. Kisten and Liel watched our moves, both of their expressions unreadable as I walked out into Kisten's backyard. It was starting to get late in the day and the sun was already low behind the trees. As soon as I closed the door, I rounded on the vampire.

"Now, tell me what the hell this is about, because if it's just to tell me you're sleeping with her or something, I swear to the Gods I'll end you." I hissed and Crispin looked away from me, not meeting my gaze anymore. He was smiling wryly and honestly looked like he'd rather be anywhere but in the backyard with me. We remained this way for a moment, and my frustration only grew as the silence dragged on.

"She made me swear to tell you before she saw me again. Cast a spell and everything," he whispered and I had to lean in to hear him. His voice held echoes of different emotions, but mostly anger. "That's why I wasn't with her when I should've been, or none of this would've happened. I should have just told you in the garden, but I–"

"Tell me what?"

"That she's pregnant," he breathed, and I froze to the ground I was standing on. I waited for him to say he was joking and laugh his cocky laugh, but he remained silent. When Crispin finally looked up to me, his expression was unreadable. "And yes, I'm... I'm the father."

"So, all that in the garden was..." I let my sentence trail, clearly not seeing the connection. He ran his hand through his golden hair, closing his eyes for a moment. "Was to tell me that?"

"She knew you hadn't forgiven yourself over me turning and she didn't know how to tell you herself, lest it felt like she was betraying you. It was her idea for me to tell you in the garden that I planted, once she and I... started getting serious. She wanted you to see that Mikael was still a part of me, even if I don't remember that life."

Crispin frowned and then chuckled. "She never told me anything about us before you did, even though I suspected there was more to her wanting to keep our relationship a secret. All she would say is that it felt wrong for her to be happy with me the way I was. Well, mostly happy."

I stood awestruck, taking in what Crispin was saying. It was like Justina to think that way, especially since I didn't know she had any sort of relationship with Crispin, much less romantic. I'd told her all my regret and guilt concerning Crispin and it would only make sense that she would feel guilty for actually preferring him the way he was now. I dropped my head into my hand, still trying to make sense of it.

"So, explain to me why you acted the way you did in the garden." I insisted, gesturing with my free hand. Crispin stiffened, clearing his throat. "I know children are a big deal to vampires, and then there's the whole issue with Justina being a sorcerer, but that doesn't explain why you didn't just tell me. Why kiss me?"

"That was, uh... mostly just me being me." He flinched as I lifted my head, my eyes glowing with power. "Mostly, Raiven. Justina wanted you to see that I wasn't just an asshole, but I... I guess some part of me wanted that too.

"I know you don't like me, and I'm not asking you to. Lucius wants us to be civil and I accept that's why he didn't want you to tell me at first. I'm not Mikael: I'm not the guy you fell for." He sounded sincere, and his voice almost sounded like he was pleading with me. I released my power as he continued. "I like my freedom, to flirt around as much as I want, to have whomever I want. But I also really do care for Justina and she gets me, accepts me in a way most people don't. I hate... I... I wish I had met her sooner."

I remained silent at this, unsure of what to say as Crispin's eyes shone with his tears. The vampire took my silence as a hopeful sign, stepping closer to me and gently touching my arm. I didn't pull back, and so he pulled me into a full hug, holding me close. After a moment, I returned his hug, and his body relaxed. He breathed deep into my hair before speaking again.

"You don't have to feel guilty anymore, Raiven. You didn't ruin me." He whispered and it wasn't until I realized his shirt was growing wet that I recognized that I was crying. I thought I had gotten over losing Mikael, that I had forgiven myself for not being there the night he was turned, but when I was forced to face who he had become, I realized how much I was still holding on to the past. I vented to Justina frequently about my frustration, my disappointment, and my guilt over Crispin, and despite that, Justina never said a word to him about his past. She waited for me to do it, waited until I was ready to try to move past it and then wanted me to see that I was wrong.

"I'm sorry, Crispin." I spoke against his chest, not ready to release him. "I...I don't think I'll ever like who you've become."

"You don't have to."

"But," I continued, pulling back slightly to look up at him, "I think I can accept it and move past it."

Crispin smiled down at me and leaned down as if to kiss me. I let him, and he placed a soft kiss on my forehead, lips barely brushing my skin. When he pulled back up, he had a gentle smile on his face and his eyes were shining with tears of relief.

"I'm guessing she can't be far along," I said, releasing him completely and wiping the tears from my eyes. Crispin stepped back from me as well, his smile evolving into a full grin, full of happiness. This only lasted a moment before his smile faded and he looked away, gripping his arm tightly.

"She's not, but do you think I..." His voice trailed off and I nodded, understanding what he wanted me to ask. Crispin had fulfilled the conditions of Justina's spell, meaning he could finally go see her for himself. The spell was probably also the reason Alex had to help Lucius carry Justina to the surface: once he had removed the door, it would have kept him from being able to approach her since he hadn't told me. I doubted that Justina's pregnancy was surprising to Kisten, and he had refrained from saying anything to respect her privacy.

"Let's go back inside. I still want to drop the evidence off at the office and Kisten can take you guys to the hospital." I insisted and saw Crispin raised his eyebrow at my suggestion, confusion on his face.

"You know you're supposed to stay together?"

"It's fine." I waved him off, turning to walk inside and after a moment, I heard him follow me. "We know this is a revenge thing, and he's not targeting us in the Coven or anything. It'll be fine."

Kisten and Liel were still in the kitchen, watching us as we returned. Liel looked to Crispin, who merely nodded at her. The dark-skinned banshee sighed, smiling as she leaned into the counter, her eyes drifting to me.

"Should've told her yesterday." She jabbed and

Crispin winced, but he was smiling as he moved to hug her.

"And forgo all the dramatic tension?" He laughed as she tried to evade his arms and I couldn't help but smile as I stood next to where Kisten sat. While Crispin tried to plant a kiss on Liel, who was actively pushing him away, I laid my hand on Kisten's shoulder and ignored the pain as he touched my hand. I looked down to find him watching me, his eyes calm. I started to remember that he had wanted to say something earlier and had just opened my mouth to ask when I was interrupted by Crispin whistling.

"Looks like Justina and I weren't the only ones hiding our relationship." He finally released Liel, who scratched him as he let her go. He hissed at her, but she merely shrugged, turning away from him. I immediately released Kisten and cleared my throat as I looked away. Crispin then turned his attention to the Alpha, leaning across the counter to be eye level with him. "Finally found a Beta? I thought you enjoyed being by yourself."

"Not all of us like to lick every cupcake first." Kisten replied smartly and Liel had to cover her mouth to hide a giggle. Crispin laughed openly, standing back up with his usual gravitas.

"What can I say? I'm a man who likes his dessert." At this Kisten stood, and it looked like he had something to say, but the two men merely locked hands. Crispin seemed genuinely happy for Kisten as he spoke. "Glad you found someone who can deal with you."

"Same to you." Kisten chuckled, releasing his hand and, heading back to the stairs, paused to kiss me. I touched my burning lips as he walked up to the bedroom to retrieve his keys, unable to help my embarrassment. Crispin laughed out loud at this, throwing his head back as he howled. Both Liel and I looked at the vampire in question, who was wiping away tears.

"God, who knew that man could be jealous?" he squeaked out through tears, wiping away the pink fluid. Upon noticing my confused expression, he did his best to quell his laughter. "I came to Lucius shortly after he became an Overseer. Kisten had been here the whole time and never once have I seen that man be with anyone, much less jealous. I thought maybe he wasn't into people, or whatever you guys call it nowadays."

"Asexual." Liel and I spoke at the same time and Crispin nodded, getting his laughter under control. He moved to turn on the kitchen light as it grew darker outside, bathing us all in light once again. Liel giggled slightly in her corner, meeting my gaze as I looked at her.

"I'll admit it, I thought that too." She shrugged, gesturing toward Crispin. "I think most people have that opinion of Kisten. He almost never talks to anyone. In the past fifty years I've been here, you're only like the second person I've ever seen Kisten hang out with."

"Who was the first?" I jumped at the question and both Crispin and Liel gave me a confused look, as if I should've known. Liel opened her mouth to answer when Kisten's arms wrapped around my middle, startling me. He cleared his throat, interrupting the banshee.

"We should get going." Kisten kissed the back of

my neck before letting go, walking toward the front door. Liel looked as if she was still going to answer my question before deciding against it, following him out. As Crispin and I trailed behind them, I couldn't help but wonder what the banshee had been going to tell me.

12

" **H** ey Raiven."

I looked up from my desk as Julia leaned over me, watching me scroll through the video on my computer. As soon as Kisten dropped me off, I passed off the screenshots and video of Justina's night at The Dream to Chris and began working on other surveillance videos that he had managed to get access to. All of the Overseers were more than willing to work with us, providing everything we needed as quickly as they could: they wanted this solved just as much as we did. I paused the video I was working on and looked over my shoulder at her.

"What's up?"

"We got in contact with Josh, that bartender from The Dream." She smiled as she spoke, and I turned around in my chair, waiting for her to continue. She leaned against the wall opposite me, a bright smile on her face. "The local division is questioning him now and Justin and Brandon are joining remotely. Hopefully, he can confirm your theory and get us that visual."

131

"The footage already does that, at least the theory part." I turned back to my computer, zooming in on the frame that I had paused. It was clearly the same man that Justina had met in The Dream and Julia gasped as she recognized the form of the man. "This is the third time I've found this man talking to a victim. He is most certainly our killer, but I can't see his face clearly in any of these videos."

"He must be doing that on purpose. He probably looks for the cameras to avoid them." Julia concluded and I nodded, letting out a frustrated sigh. Technology had advanced so much since I had started doing this and still we couldn't identify a killer from a video. Julia shook her head, clearly sharing my sentiment. "We would need video of the first victim, before he would have thought to hide his face."

"Yeah, but we don't have a connection for that first crime." I sighed, leaning back in my chair again as I recited the details. "That was the one that took place in a coffee shop in broad daylight. Eight people died, including the cashiers. The only survivor was the manager, who was in his office with the door closed. Guess he didn't think to check there. Or didn't care."

"Yeah, and as far as we've been able to discover, not one of those victims had visited a bar, club or similar environment leading up to the massacre. Even the café's surveillance doesn't show this guy arriving before the killing, so he must've met his target somewhere else," Julia continued and I nodded. She frowned, clearly trying to piece the puzzle together in her mind. "But if they met on the street or something, we'd have no way to tell who the target was. And now that I think about it, why don't we have a video of the killings?"

"The camera was destroyed during the attack, remember?" I reminded her and she closed her eyes in thought. The local division had been so upset about it that they almost didn't want to tell us. We still hadn't been able to determine if the camera being destroyed was premeditated, or simply a consequence of the violent attack.

"So, we really have nothing about the first one, not even the gender of his target."

"Nope, because he seems to go after men too." I stood, turning to face her, walking away from my desk to find Chris. Julia followed behind me as I continued my train of thought. "We also need to determine why his switch was suddenly flipped. Why did he suddenly decide to start killing? The way this guy gets turned down, insulted or humiliated, there's no way the café was the first time that ever happened."

"Because he got away with the first one?" Julia offered and I shrugged, not slowing my stride.

"Possibly. We weren't called on until the third killing and now, with Justina's attack, we're up to six. The time between killings has been on a steady decline and the number of victims on a steady incline, so he's definitely been getting more confident. We're really on a tight schedule to find him before he leaves again." I shook my head as I knocked before opening the door, letting Julia walk in before me. Chris was still running the woman's face through our database and smiled at us as we walked in.

"Still searching," he glanced at his computer, watching the images fly by. "I've checked if she was human as well as all of our suspected races. I didn't get a match, so we can rule out her being the killer."

"Not yet," I interrupted him, remembering what LeAlexende had told me at the hospital. "It's possible our killer could be a hybrid and we can't rule out that this woman and the guy may be a pair."

"But she hasn't shown up in any other locations, has she? Just the male, from what I've noticed."

"Can't rule out that she's a shapeshifter species," I insisted and Chris nodded, seeing my line of thinking. "It is safe to assume that this would be her actual appearance, as Justina recognized her when she arrived. She was too friendly with the man at The Dream for that to be the first time they met."

"Alright, I'll shift my focus to shapeshifting species." Chris paused his current search and started to change the parameters in the search bar. I nodded as he started the new search, more pictures flashing next to our sample image. He turned to Julia and me, waving us out of his office. "There's no need to stand around, I'll call a meeting as soon as I get a match. Although if she is a shapeshifter, I'll also need to..."

Julia and I had to hide our laughter as we left, closing the door behind us. Chris was by far the most excited when it came to Supernaturals and was our team's current specialist on current affairs. If he had known how old I was, I'm sure he would've loved to sit me down and bleed me dry of my knowledge. However, only the Director knew the truth, and as far as my team was concerned, I was human like the rest of them. My official role was as a history specialist; since so many Supernaturals outlived humans, it was considered important to understand their hidden history and it helped to hide why I knew as much as I did about them.

"Hey..." Julia stopped walking, her expression lost in thought behind me. "Just a thought, but wouldn't he stay until he could kill Justina?"

"What do you mean?" I asked, and she gestured in the empty air between us.

"I mean, wouldn't he be upset about not getting to finish her off?" she reasoned, and I crossed my arms, turning to face her. "I mean, he's always successfully killed his target since he started. That's why he's kept doing it: he's had a taste of retribution and he loved it."

"Except Justina, who somehow survived." I added and she nodded, still lost in her own thoughts.

"Right. I don't think he'll leave town until he gets her. It's almost a matter of pride at this point. He managed to kill more than fifteen people last time, but this time he couldn't even kill a single witch?" Julia had a point and I hummed as I thought of a response.

"That is possible, but..."

"Um, Raiven?" Julia and I were interrupted as the receptionist called out to me, and she was a bit frazzled as she stepped back into the office. I gave her a concerned look and she tried to pull herself together, her voice still shaking. "Um, the Alpha is here to see you. He says it's important."

I groaned out loud, rolling my eyes. I had told Kisten to call me before he came back to pick me up, but it was obvious that my preferences weren't on the table. Julia continued back to her desk as I walked up front with the receptionist, seeing Kisten in the lobby by himself. Both Crispin and Liel had been impatient to see Justina and I would imagine that, now that they had delivered the video, the pair was no longer interested in being with me or Kisten.

"Raiven." Kisten didn't give me a moment to say a word, immediately grabbing me. His tone was worried and his eyes were swirling with power. "We need to get back to the Coven *now*."

"Shh, Kisten, not so loud," I dropped my voice and, giving the receptionist a smile, moved Kisten to the opposite side of the lobby. He looked over to her and back to me, confused by my reaction. I leaned him down, speaking to him in a hushed tone. "No one here knows that I'm more than human, that's part of my agreement."

"The woman is at the Coven. The one from the video," Kisten whispered and I raised my eyebrows in surprise. "She was asking Lucius for protection. Says she knows who did this to Justina."

"Then I need to get Brandon and bring her in."

"Lucius has her locked up in the Basement." Kisten said urgently and I suddenly understood his impatience and concern. The Basement was only meant to hold those Lucius had deemed a danger to others and having her down there meant he would not give her up so easily. I sighed, frustrated by this news.

"Why?"

"He doesn't want to risk that she's the one who did this. He says he'll only give her up to you guys once you have the man in custody as well." Kisten glanced toward the receptionist before looking at me again. "She's a lamia, originally from the west coast, but she never checked in with me when she arrived."

"How do you know she's there then?" From the

way he was speaking, it clearly wasn't Lucius who told him, and Eve never would've offered that up for free, especially if it would help me. Kisten groaned, clearly not seeing how it mattered.

"Aurel called me." His tone was annoyed and worried and he gestured toward the door. "We need to go, before Lucius does something to her and you lose the only lead you have. He's beyond pissed."

"Okay, okay," I sighed, and Kisten fidgeted, clearly in a hurry to leave. I gave him a curt nod as I walked back toward the office. "Give me a second to update Brandon and I'll come with you. I'll only be a moment."

"Hurry." Kisten called after me as I walked back through the security door, clearly antsy in the chair as he sat. I made directly for the interrogation room, where Brandon and Justin were still questioning Josh. The poor boy looked terrified on the hologram and was fidgeting as he spoke. I couldn't blame him for his fear; it was likely that Lucius could blame him for what happened to Justina, even though he had no part other than being present. However, he was a shapeshifter and therefore a part of Kisten's pack, so there was no way Kisten would allow any harm to come to him, regardless of Lucius' anger.

I knocked on the door, getting Brandon's attention. He glanced back at the glass and, despite not being able to see me, I knocked against it. He excused himself from the projection and quietly slid out the door to see who it was. He clearly was not expecting it to be me, as his tone was surprised as he spoke.

"Raiven? I'm in the middle of—"

"Lucius has the woman," I said, making it evident that there was no time to waste. Brandon cursed under his breath and he stepped out into the hallway as I continued. "She's a lamia who's not from this area, so he refuses to release her until we have the guy in custody."

"But we don't know if she's involved beyond Justina." he reasoned, echoing what Chris had said earlier and I sighed, slightly frustrated at their naivete. Must be nice.

"I know, but Lucius is not going to risk it. Lamias are shapeshifters who can look like anyone, so it would be hard to be sure. Besides, I don't think Lucius cares if she's involved beyond Justina: she's involved *with* Justina." I countered and he cursed again, clearly frustrated. "I just came to let you know the state of things. I'm heading there now to see if I can convince him to at least let me talk to her."

"Go. The kid's agreed to give us access to his memories and we're just waiting on the tech. Hopefully, we can get the visual of him soon and find the bastard." Brandon agreed and I turned and left, almost jogging through the office as I made it back to Kisten. Julia called my name as I ran past, but I ignored her as I stepped back into the lobby. Without a word, Kisten stood and opened the door for me, and I instantly shivered as the cold air hit me, not expecting it as I looked around for his car.

"Where..." I didn't get to finish speaking as Kisten padded up next to me, fully shifted into his leopard form. He rubbed his head against my hand and lay down, clearly waiting for me to get on. Kisten must've been truly worried about what Lucius would do, as it was dangerous for him to roam the city in animal form. He was one of the few shifters who could probably do so without being spotted, but it was still only something he did when he was in a hurry. I hopped onto the giant cat, grabbing hold of his fur tightly and pressing myself against him. He stood and took off into the night, heading for the Landing.

As the wind rushed past us in the cold night air, I couldn't help but hope we could reach Lucius before the worst happened.

13

I leapt off Kisten's back as we arrived at the Coven and he shifted back to human as I started down the stairs. I wasn't surprised when Aurel and Grace met us in the hallway, hurrying along behind us as we rushed past them.

"Lucius and Evalyn are currently out, they just left Nirvana." Aurel sounded out of breath as we reached the second set of stairs, Kisten and me not pausing as we continued down. Nirvana was one of Lucius' clubs on the other side of town and it would take him a good while to get back to the Coven. "I don't know how long it'll be before they get here. Lucius is absolutely furious—"

"I'm not waiting, he can punish me later," I interrupted, letting Kisten pass me so he could open the door to the Basement. Only one of the Three, or someone with Lucius' permission, could open the door, so I was truly lucky to have Kisten on my side. "There was no telling what Lucius will do to her once he comes back, and I'm not willing to risk losing my only lead to catching the one who hurt Justina."

"Alpha..." Grace's voice trailed off as she fidgeted

140

behind Aurel, and Kisten turned to face her as he finished opening the door. His expression softened and he nodded curtly as he swung the door open. Grace sighed with relief, clutching her shirt as she quickly ascended the stairs. I was confused by their interaction but turned to enter the dungeon.

When we arrived in the Basement, it was as if I had stepped into a different era. The walls were lit with torches and before me was a hallway lined with stone cells, iron bars holding in the inhabitants. I had never been in the Basement and even now, I wanted nothing more than to run back up to the safety of the surface as Grace had done. The medieval atmosphere of the dungeon only brought back horrible memories of my first few years away from Mother and fleeing her Hunters.

Steeling myself, I quietly walked past the cells, only glancing into each in the hope of seeing the woman. I knew most of these people deserved to be down here: to be in the Basement was considered a fate worse than death. Anyone down here had either hurt someone else in the area, or betrayed Lucius' trust. They would be down here until the day they died, or until the day Lucius finally decided to kill them.

"There," Aurel pointed to a cell in front of me and I could hear a woman crying as we got closer. "That's where she is."

"Kisten, go back up. See if you can talk some sense into Lucius once he arrives." Kisten obeyed, nodding as he went back, disappearing into darkness as he ascended the stairs. I stopped in front of the cell Aurel had pointed out, with the lich hovering close behind me. It was indeed the woman from the video, but her lower half was no longer human. She leaned against the wall, tears evident on her face as she sat coiled on her beautiful brown tail. Her scales flexed as she looked at me, a sad expression on her face.

"Are you here to punish me?" she asked softly, barely lifting her head from the stone. She leaned against it again after I shook my head. "You should be. I don't deserve kindness."

"What's your name?" I dropped my voice, doing my best to sound professional and polite. She dragged herself from the wall, slithering across the floor to meet me at the bars. She raised herself to my height and we looked deeply into one another's eyes. She must've trusted what she saw there, because she dropped herself back down, sitting on her coils again before she spoke.

"Irida."

"Why are you in Decver?"

"I'm here with my boyfri–" She stopped herself, sighing as she began to cry softly. I grabbed the bars that separated us, pulling myself closer to the barrier.

"Is he the one who hurt Justina?" She visibly flinched as I said this, and her next response was low and full of her tears.

"Yes... no... yes," She looked up at me again, tears flowing freely down her face. Her top was soaked, indicating that she had been crying for a while, probably since Aurel had brought her down here. "I... you have to help me. Please."

"Why do you need help?" I asked softly, dropping to my knees to meet her gaze. She looked away, as if she couldn't bear to look at me. She started to openly sob again, the sounds echoing through the stone hallways. I pushed my hand through the bars and she took it, squeezing it tightly as she tried to calm herself down. "Has he threatened to hurt you? To kill you, too?"

"No... yes," she stammered. "Not outright, just... I swear, I didn't know what he was doing at the time, it wasn't until Justina that I realized—"

She stopped as the door to the Basement flew open and, from the electricity in the air, I knew Lucius had arrived. I released her hand as I stood, and she slithered back into her corner, terrified of the Overseer. I readied myself as Lucius came into view, both Evalyn and Kisten trailing behind him. His blue eyes were practically glowing, and his calm face did little to hide his obvious anger.

"Raiven," he stated my name and I fought the urge to kneel, ignoring his silent command. Eve looked at me shocked, her gaze turning to Lucius as I disobeyed him. The Overseer continued up to me, standing over me as I remained on my feet, refusing to back down from his gaze. Kisten and Eve stopped a distance away from us, standing side by side. "You cannot take her."

"I am not trying to," I fought my legs as they tried to buckle, and I stomped my foot, planting my legs apart. Lucius' expression did not change, but the electricity in the air changed as he shifted the charge. "I am questioning her."

"There is nothing to question," he stated, and the lamia whimpered in her cell, understanding that he would not help her. I glared back at Lucius as I summoned my own power, my green eyes starting to swirl as the stone around us began to shake. Lucius raised his eyebrow at my obvious threat. "Are you challenging me, Raiven?"

"I am." I growled, the air growing heavy as I summoned my power to challenge his. It was starting to get difficult to breathe between the electricity and dense air, but I would not back down to Lucius. My own behavior was slightly surprising to me, but I pushed these thoughts away as I spoke. "I *will not* allow you to hurt her."

"*You will obey me.*" Lucius' face changed, visibly showing the anger he had kept hidden behind his facade and all of our hair stood on end as the charge in the air increased. I raised more of my own power, the stone beneath our feet shifting and changing as I glared. Lucius scowled at me and even Eve backed away from him, almost cowering behind Kisten as she started to lose her grip on her human form. Her horns started to peek out from her hair as she whimpered, but Kisten ignored her, keeping his eyes on me. I could tell from his expression that he was clearly worried, but I was unwavering in my conviction.

"*I will not.*" I insisted, refusing to look away from Lucius and the glow in his eyes grew brighter with his anger. "And you cannot make me. I *will* question her and I *will* get the information I need."

Lucius seemed ready to raise his hand against me and I readied myself to retaliate. I heard Aurel behind me step back, clearly wanting to get away from the struggle between me and Lucius. Eve shared his sentiments, grabbing Kisten for protection as her tail appeared behind her.

"**Rai–**"

"Lucius!" Kisten interrupted him and Lucius paused, his eyes still locked on mine. Kisten took this as a good sign and took a step closer, forcing Eve to release him. His movements were slow and cautious

144

as he reached out to the Overseer. "This is not how we agreed to do things. Raiven is just trying to do her job."

"Justina—"

"Will be fine." Kisten insisted, still moving closer to his friend. The glow in Lucius' eyes wavered for a moment, but his gaze didn't move from mine. I backed down a bit, recalling my power as Kisten continued. "Blood for Blood, but not this. If you kill or harm this woman, she'll never catch the one who actually attacked Justina. This is not how we wanted to do things; we agreed to never do things Her way."

Lucius closed his eyes at the mention of Mater Vitae and he seemed as if he were taking Kisten's words to heart. His eyes still glowed when he opened them again, but the charge in the air had lessened. I still met his eyes evenly, waiting to see what he would do. He glanced at Irida, who cowered under his gaze and she shifted further into the corner, as if trying to escape him. His eyes softened for a moment, and I ventured a chance to speak.

"By all means, keep her. She wanted your protection, anyway," I suggested, and Lucius returned his attention to me as his eyes narrowed. I fought the urge to cower and took a deep breath. "I just want to question her and get whatever I can from her."

"Then question her." Lucius relented, standing against the wall across from her cell and motioning Evalyn and Kisten to his side. Kisten immediately moved to his friend's side and Eve reluctantly obeyed, leaning against him as he wrapped his arm around her. Taking a deep breath, I turned to face Irida again, dropping to my knees.

"Irida." She jumped as if struck when I called her

name, and I spoke more softly. "Please, Irida, I need you to tell me what you can."

"I... I can't," she whined, hiding deeper in her corner as she started to sob again. "He has a spell on me, I can't act against him. I can't even say his name anymore."

"He's a spellcaster?" I coaxed and she nodded, turning her teary eyes to me. She seemed to have some determination despite her fear, and she was trying to figure out what she could say. "A witch, or a warlock?"

"I swear I didn't know. I thought he was a normal human," she moaned, trying her best to speak between sobs as she chose her words carefully. "I didn't know he was using me to do... to do... those things..."

"Wait," Kisten interrupted me, and she jumped at the sound of his voice, turning away again. "He controlled you?"

"Yes." she wailed, the answer sending her into another crying fit. The air charged around us again and I turned anxiously to Lucius. His grip on Eve had tightened and he was looking at Irida darkly as she cried. I was stunned into silence as she wailed, her tears having long since dried from the lack of water. I glanced at Kisten and I knew we were having the same thoughts: only witches had the ability to control other beings against their will. It was rare for one to be able to control humans, and even worse if they could do it to other Supernaturals.

"I didn't know what he was doing, I didn't know he was using me for my mother's ability." Irida suddenly flung herself into the wall, the sound of her body colliding with the stone causing a cracking sound that made my stomach turn. Kisten didn't hesitate as he threw open the bars and rushed in to check on her. Her arm was bleeding, and Kisten reached for the sheet that lay on the simple bed, tearing it to make a bandage. Irida was covering her mouth as she tried to calm herself down, and she looked at me, begging me with her expression. It was clear that it was the spell that had caused her to hurt herself and she was frantic to find the right words. "He said we were going on a road trip and I didn't think anything of it. Ju... Here... I... I realized when I saw Justina..."

"You stopped yourself," I finished and she nodded, covering her mouth again. Her beautiful brown eyes were red from her tears and she pulled in a shaky breath. She was truly trying her best to help me, despite the obvious danger to herself. I curled my fingers in anger as Kisten checked her arm to make sure nothing was broken. I had to close my eyes and take a deep breath before I could speak again. "That's why Justina survived, why no major organs were damaged. You were able to overpower him once you realized."

"To overcome means to be aware. I was never aware of what was happening. I think he always waited until... I only realized he had taken precautions when I tried to tell Justina," she lamented, slithering away from Kisten and back up to me, taking my hands again. Her grip was desperate and my fingers ached from how tightly she squeezed them together. "She... tried to help me. That's how she got hurt. She was trying to... stop me while he was trying to regain control... Eventually, when they came to the door, he gave up and Justina told me to hide."

"Where have you been all this time?" I spoke soothingly, shifting her grip and stroking the back of her hands. Irida hiccupped as she tried to control her emotions, chancing a glance at Lucius. He was merely watching her blankly and she returned her gaze to me. I hushed her, trying to help keep her calm. "It's okay, just tell me."

"I've... I've been here the whole time," she admitted, her body shaking from fear. "I didn't know how to leave. I don't even know where *here* is, so I stayed hidden in Justina's room. I came out when I knew he was trying to control me again. I knew there were people at the door and I needed someone to help me.

"Please, I don't want to hurt anyone, I don't want to kill anyone!" she screamed, grabbing my hands and squeezing them painfully again as she begged, even turning her gaze to Lucius. "Kill me if you have to, but don't let him use me anymore! Please!"

I turned to look at Lucius, who had turned away from her completely. Kisten was watching his friend as he stepped out of the cell, all waiting to see what he would say. I understood that he had to feel torn: as one of the First, he understood what it was like to be forced to do things against your will, including killing those you cared about. However, his own anger toward her for what she had done was fighting his compassion and I wasn't sure which would win out. I wanted to believe Lucius would be reasonable, but emotions weren't always logical.

"She will stay down here, far from where he can reach her," he stated, his voice still full of anger. "If he attempts to control her, I will kill her, as she asked."

"I'll find him before then," I swore, releasing Irida's hands and turning to face the vampire. He met my gaze, clearly still upset with me for my earlier insubordination. "When he is caught, you will release her, and you can take your anger out on him. He is to blame, not her."

"Of course," he agreed and Kisten sighed, moving to comfort the lamia as she started crying again, this time with relief. Eve watched the whole exchange silently, chancing a glance up to Lucius as her horns and tail retreated. The vampire ignored her however, keeping his eyes on me. "Do you have any leads?"

"We know what he looks like, thanks to Josh, and now we know he's a witch." I revealed, glancing back to the sobbing woman. She was limp in Kisten's arms, her shoulders still shaking from her predicament. "He won't leave without her, so we know he has to still be in Decver. She's his only means of killing those who slight him. If he could've done it himself, he would've a long time ago."

Lucius nodded as I continued. "He has to know she's here somewhere. After all, it's easier to control someone if you're near them and he must not realize she's underground. He must've been at the shops earlier, if he tried before she revealed herself."

"Keeping her down here is the safest," Kisten added, releasing her and standing as he closed the cell door. "It's not the most comfortable place, but she'll be far from the surface and we can make sure she's safe. He would have to be inside The Dream to even think about getting close enough."

"Which means we could lure him in." Lucius suggested and I nodded in agreement.

"Yeah, we could easily have someone waiting for him." I glanced behind me at the lamia, who had dragged herself back to her corner, facing away from us. It must've been heartbreaking to have been betrayed in the way he had used her, and I started to grow angrier on her behalf. "He'll probably try to avoid coming in, but eventually he'll give in to what we want. Even if he wants to take a hostage to bargain, he knows he'll have to come here."

"What makes you so sure?" Eve asked, giving me a look of disbelief. I closed my eyes, sighing heavily. "It would be smarter to leave her and find someone else."

"Not many can overcome magical barriers, it's an exceedingly rare ability," I reminded her and she refused to accept my explanation, still shaking her head. "If he had been able to find someone before, he would've probably started killing sooner. His ability to control her is probably the only thing he's good at,"

"Even if we know who she is, there's nothing to keep him from using her abilities for himself as he has been. A lamia is hard to keep track of, and he's been using that to his advantage this whole time. By not having her check in with local Alphas, he's basically been smuggling her across the Governances.

"It's also a matter of pride and revenge against her and Justina," I continued, glancing again at the poor woman. "She finally resisted him and cost him his kill. He will use her to kill Justina, even if he kills her afterwards."

Eve looked as if she was going to continue arguing with me, but Lucius silenced her, squeezing her in his grip. His eyes were on Irida as she sobbed quietly in her corner, trying her best to stay out of our way.

"Our people or yours?" he asked, and I sighed, running my hands over my hair.

"Both would be best. Plant a member of my team and a member of the Coven in the club, working together. He won't be afraid if approached by a human, but having a Supernatural as back-up would be mandatory. This guy is too dangerous and too cunning if he can control other Supernaturals, so only someone of the Coven would be strong enough to resist him."

Lucius nodded and looked to Aurel, who stepped back to join us. He merely bowed his head to Lucius and started towards the stairs that would take him above ground. Lucius released Eve and started after Aurel, but was stopped by Kisten.

"A moment?" he asked and Lucius agreed, motioning for Eve to go up without him. She hesitated as if to argue, but decided against it, merely glaring as Kisten walked further into the Basement with Lucius. She then turned her attention to me and glared.

"I bet you just love this, getting to be the one to solve this case," she hissed and I ignored her, starting toward the stairs. I'd had enough of the dungeon and while I felt bad about leaving Irida alone, I couldn't stand the idea of staying. Eve stomped after me, her anger radiating off her. "It should've been the local team; it should've been *me*."

"There's no glory here, Evalyn." I huffed, climbing the dark stairs. She scoffed behind me, turning me around once we reached the Coven. Her horns had started to appear again and I met her gaze evenly, despite the heat from her touch. However, I knew the heat from her had nothing to do with the Oath and everything to do with her own flames. I glared at her evenly, almost daring her to use her powers on me; all I needed was an excuse. "All that matters is stopping this lunatic so he can't hurt anyone ever again. Doesn't matter who does it."

Eve merely hissed at me and I pulled myself from

her grip, climbing all the way up to the surface, checking my phone for a signal. She paused as if she was going to follow me, but decided against it, turning down another hallway as I closed the door. I leaned against the wall as I waited for a signal, my thoughts turning to poor Irida.

I'll get him, for both of you. I swore, calling the office as soon as my service returned. *He's going to regret this dearly.*

14

After putting the finishing touches to my plan with Brandon and the team, I hung up, closing my eyes as I leaned against the building. I glanced at my phone as it reminded me of its low battery, and I peeled myself from the wall. I walked to my car still in the parking lot, exhaustion hitting me as I sat inside.

I started her up and plugged in my phone, closing my eyes again as I waited for Julia to arrive. I had told her what Aurel looked like and to meet him in front of The Dream, but I wasn't sure if he'd be there. She was supposed to call me if she couldn't find him and I lifted my phone to check the time.

The bright screen told me it was 9:45pm, and I knew The Dream had opened a short while ago. I doubted our suspect would come tonight, but we couldn't rule out the possibility of it happening. Thanks to her refusal of him, he had to know that Irida had betrayed him, and depending on how impatient he was, it was possible that he would do whatever it took to find her.

I looked up as the door to the Coven opened and I

saw Kisten step out, a soft look on his face. I had been curious as to what he wanted to talk to Lucius about, but it was obvious that it was private, and not something he wanted to share. My thoughts drifted to his annoyed behavior while Crispin and Liel were at his house, and I readied myself to face him as he looked around for me.

"Here," I turned off my car and opened my door, motioning him toward me. Kisten walked toward me and I was slightly worried as he pulled me out of my car and closed the door. He wrapped his arm around my waist, and I glanced around anxiously. "What are you doing? What if someone sees—"

I was interrupted as he leaned down to kiss me, and for the first time, no intense heat and pain followed. Surprised, but not wanting to let the moment pass, I wrapped my arms around him as he pulled me closer. I let my tongue dance across his lips, enticing him to let me in. He did, and I almost moaned at the sensation of our tongues sliding against one another without the usual pain distracting me. He almost seemed to be trying to drink me in and I let him, clinging to him as we kissed.

"Kisten," I gasped, pulling back after what seemed like eternity. "Why didn't the Oath affect me?"

"Till sunrise." He smiled, hugging me close as if I'd disappear if he let me go. His voice caressed my skin as he spoke softly against it. "Until sunrise, you can be mine."

So that's what you asked Lucius. I smiled, hugging him tightly, silently thanking Lucius for this small gift. "How did you talk him into it? How did you talk *Eve* into it?"

"Being honest. I told him I wanted to make you my mate and court you correctly." Kisten shrugged as he pulled me towards the back door of The Dream, and I pulled against him slightly. "Asked for one night free of the Oath to convince you and he agreed. I'd imagine Eve is not happy about it."

"But why are we..." I started, but Kisten pulled me inside and I found myself drowned in bodies and loud music. He pulled me towards the bar and sat me in his lap.

"You are in dire need of a distraction. Let Aurel and your team handle the case for one night." He waved to the bartender, another member of the pack. She bounced toward him and smiled, clearly recognizing her Alpha. "Vodka for the lady and gin for me."

"Of course, Kisten." She winked at him, a gleam in her eye as she looked at me. As she turned to make our drinks, I tried to slide out of his lap but he wrapped his arms around me to keep me still. Kisten then pulled me higher so that I could know how happy he was to have me there. Just feeling how hard he was, that hardness pressing into my thigh, made me catch my breath.

"I like you in my lap." His voice caressed my ear as the bartender set our glasses down. Her expression told me that she understood her Alpha's intentions and she smiled at me brightly.

"First round's on me, as thanks for earlier," The girl giggled and I watched as her brown eyes shone brightly, and I faintly caught the scent of the ocean as she took my hand. "You take good care of him."

"Do you have to make it so obvious?" I sipped on my glass as she released me and he laughed. I hummed as I refused to look at him, the song drifting into another similar sounding tune.

"They'll all know soon enough." He reasoned, kissing my skin and I sighed with relief. I almost missed the pain but couldn't deny the simple pleasure of feeling his lips on my skin without it. It was as if he was trying to drive me crazy, giving me a taste of what it would be like if I were his mate... if I would say yes to him like he knew I wanted to.

Trying to clear my head of those thoughts, I turned my gaze to the sea of movement. If I hadn't known we were in a club, I could've almost sworn this was some type of sex ceremony. I had never been inside a club like this: even when Lucius required me to help, I mostly stayed outside, helping with security. The intense energy and movement was new to me and I wondered what the appeal of the environment was.

Out of the corner of my eye, I saw a young man walking in the front door and I couldn't help but tense up as he glanced around the club. He spotted me and made a beeline for my seat and as he grew closer, I recognized that he looked nothing like our suspect. Once he saw the Alpha holding me in his lap, he tried to mask his actions and sat two seats away, his eyes still on me. I couldn't help but laugh and give him a wink as I took another sip of my drink. I leaned back against Kisten so he could hear me over the noise. "No competition, hmm?"

"I would certainly hope not." He glanced behind us, looking for my pursuer. Upon noticing the man staring at me, he smiled, his fangs visible as his eyes swirled with power. The man quickly left his seat and I glared at Kisten, hitting him playfully.

"You did that on purpose. Poor guy probably wet his pants."

"I'd buy his fucking drinks if he didn't." He laughed darkly, and I gave him a surprised look. I had never heard such vulgar language from Kisten before and it sounded so foreign in his voice. Having finished his own, he took my drink and nearly drained it. He waved for the bartender to refill them, sliding some bills underneath the glasses. "I saw the way you winked at him."

"Whatever." I turned to my re-filled drink, taking a long swig while trying not to ask the burning question in my mind. Curiosity finally won and I dropped my drink into my lap. "Kisten."

"Yes?"

"Were... are you jealous?"

"Of?" He turned me in his lap so he could see my face, but I gazed into my drink as I avoided looking at him. I couldn't help but remember the dark look he had given Crispin and I suspected Liel had filled him in on the truth about my past with the vampire. His behavior afterwards also appeared to show his jealousy, but I wasn't sure.

"Never mind..."

"Not really," he answered, raising my face to his. He searched my eyes with his before pulling me into another blissful kiss. He was smiling softly when he pulled back, eyes still locked with mine. "Crispin isn't Mikael. You don't like it, but it seems you've accepted that the person you loved is dead. There's nothing to be jealous of."

"Oh." I mumbled, finishing down my drink. Of course Kisten would think that way: with Crispin's relationship with Justina, it was clear that we weren't involved in any way. My mind went back to the other person Liel and Crispin said they had seen Kisten be around and I began to wonder if that had been Kisten's first love.

"Kisten, who did you—"

"Time to dance." he interrupted me, downing his second drink and spinning around in his seat. I hummed with annoyance: it was obvious he was trying to avoid my question, just as he had stopped Liel from telling me earlier.

"But..." I started to protest, but he was out of the seat and pulling me to the dance floor. He swung me so I was in front of him and wrapped his arm around my waist while his other hand gripped mine. His front was pressed along the length of my back, hips intimately touching.

"Tonight's about me and you. Let's enjoy it," he leaned forward as he whispered in my ear, his voice full of darker things. "No Eve, no Crispin, no case: *just us.*"

Since I had never danced before, he started out slow and I followed the line of his body. Once I grasped the movements, it felt as if the beat began to move me; soon I was dancing against him on my own. Kisten whipped me around to face him, still gripping my hand as if I'd run away at my first chance. After a while, I wasn't sure why he was so worried: I was strangely enjoying myself with this new way of dancing.

Soon, however, I got bored with his way of movement: he was keeping it simple, swaying, and a little rubbing. However, this simple dance was not what I wanted, and not what I craved. I did a slow twist of my hips that ground my groin against his, humming with my pleasure. His chartreuse eyes lit with fire as I continued my grinding and twisting.

"Be careful, Raiven." I shuddered slightly as he leaned down and his breath caressed my ear. I flicked out my tongue to tease his earlobe and traced it down the side of his face until I found the warm crevice of his mouth.

"You know I like to play with fire." I smiled, twisting myself again and he growled, planting a kiss on my forehead. "You can't expect me to stop now."

"Is that so?" Once again, our mouths joined in the darkness of the club as he grasped my hips, moving me so that I ground myself against him. With him controlling my movements, the feeling became more intense and I moaned into his kiss. His tongue rolled in and out of mine, mimicking what he wanted to do with my body. I barely noticed as he moved us across the dance floor towards the far wall and I connected with it softly. Kisten gently stroked my face before kissing me again, pressing himself into me. His body was crushing me against the wall, but I loved every second of this pain-free contact. I moved to wrap my arms around his neck, but he stopped me, pinning my hands to the wall above me as I moaned into his kiss. He pulled back after a moment, his eyes now swirling with his lust and desire.

"Decide now, Raiven. Do you want this... want me?" he panted, still trying to exercise some of his careful control. "Because I can't take much more before I decide for you."

I couldn't begin to articulate my need for him. I had wanted Kisten from the moment I had met him, and my desire and love had only grown over the past three years I had been in Decver. I knew this was all to tempt me into being his Beta, but we both already knew what my answer would be.

"Kisten," I began, but I froze against him, tension ringing off my body. Kisten lightly shook me but my mind was completely blank with surprise. "Oh, no-no-no."

"What?" Kisten saw the many emotions flash across my face as my eyes rested on the person at the bar. He leaned across it, his eyes searching as my co-worker sat next to him, facing the bartender. Julia's hair was beautifully done and her dress was revealing enough to make me blush, but it was the lich next to her that had my attention.

"Aurel." I could see Kisten's confusion as I began to look for a way to escape, to get away from where he could see me. I felt as if Aurel would be able to pick me out of the squirming crowd, despite how unrealistic that was.

"What's wrong? He's supposed to be here, remember?" Kisten's confusion was obvious in his voice and I squirmed to free my hands from his grip. He held me tightly, however, still refusing to let me go.

"I don't want him to see me like this." I begged and Kisten's eyes darkened with jealousy again as he looked down at me. His growl was barely contained when he spoke again, pressing me into the wall more.

"And why is that? Something I should know about you two?"

"No, I don't..." I stumbled over the words as I tried to explain myself, still twisting to get away. I looked away to the floor but Kisten pinned me closer against the wall, making it evident that he would not let me leave. I moaned as he assaulted my neck, playfully biting and licking me. "Please, Kisten, I just don't want him to see us, this isn't how I want to tell him."

Kisten paused for a moment as he considered my words, his hand tightening around my wrists as he hesitated. Without releasing me, we made our way through the moving bodies along the wall and I knew he meant to take the door leading to the Coven. It was as if the crowd was pushing us where we wanted to go: we floated along the wall, effortlessly moving toward the door. Reaching our escape, Kisten silently opened it and we slipped past the barrier and into the dark stairwell.

As soon as we were in the Coven, Kisten slammed me into the door, assaulting me once again with his mouth as he pinned me against it. The sound of me hitting the door was drowned out by the loud music on the other side and I knew that no one inside was any the wiser to my plight. I moaned openly, my hand grasping his hair as he kissed and bit my neck, working his way down to my collarbone.

"Want to tell me what that was?" he growled, never ceasing his assault on me. I struggled to speak in between my own gasps and moans.

"Aurel, he wants me for his harem." I managed and Kisten paused, standing up straight to meet my gaze. His eyes swirled with a mix of desire and anger and this time, I knew his jealousy was real, unlike the mix of emotions he had shown towards Crispin.

"And?" He spat the word out, no longer touching me sensually but keeping me against the door. I had never seen Kisten angry and I was starting to wish I never had; he loomed over me, his presence and anger filling the stairway as he waited for my answer. I felt like prey as he kept me pinned, and I already knew I would not be able to escape him unless I was willing to hurt him.

"Aurel doesn't take rejection well," I whispered, looking away from Kisten's intense gaze. "I told him I didn't want that, but I haven't told him how I feel about you."

"And?" Kisten pressed, leaning down close to my ear again, breathing his words into me as I shuddered. I could still sense the anger in his words, but it had lessened with my admission and his desire was winning him over again. "How *do* you feel about me?"

"I..." I paused, knowing what he wanted to hear. There was so much more than just how I felt, but that was all Kisten seemed to care about. He was willing to risk everything to keep me at his side, and could I claim to care as much as I did if I wouldn't do the same? Things could be worked out with my job and Kisten was right. I doubted the new Director would be willing to let me go so easily, and as far as the Hunters... he was the Alpha to a First and that made him a target regardless. I closed my eyes, moaning softly as I made up my mind.

"*Kisten...*"

"Tell me." he whispered, taking a deep breath as he breathed in the scent of our combined desire. I knew he wanted to hear me say it, to finally hear me admit it to him. I reached up, cradling Kisten's face with my hands and he let me, his eyes still angry as he waited for my answer. I sighed as I enjoyed the feeling of his skin in my hands, and I couldn't help but stroke his cheek with my thumbs.

"I want you." I breathed. His expression softened at my words, and I whispered my next phrase. "I love you."

"Good." I yelped as he scooped me up and started carrying me down the hallway to his room. I had never been to Kisten's room in the Coven before and barely saw the insignia on the door as he opened it and swung us in. He closed the door with his foot and immediately carried me to the bed, barely giving me time to look around. He laid me on it gently, leaning over me as he stroked my face and I wrapped my arms around him, saying the first thing that came to mind.

"Kiss me."

15

I allowed myself to get lost in his kiss, purely concentrating on how wonderful it felt to have him holding me, kissing me, after all the time we had waited. His arm was firm around my waist, one of my hands tangled in his brown waves while he kissed me, our tongues dancing in passion's embrace. Pulling me closer, he rubbed his groin against mine, and a delicious warmth exploded through my body before settling back in my lower region. I let out a gasp and clung to him as he did it again.

"How badly do you want me, Raiven?" Seeing that masculine smirk on his face, hearing the thickness in his voice, only proved to intensify my desire and I felt as if I might die if I didn't have him in me at that moment. Knowing the effect his words had on me, he held me against his body, and rubbed our groins against each other again. He continued using his body to pin me to the bed until I thought I would fall through it.

"How badly do you want me to be inside you?" Kisten whispered against my skin, enjoying his dominance over me. His words danced over me, flowing like water. "Tell me, Raiven, I want to hear you say you want me."

"This much." I pushed him off me and he let me, lying back on his bed. I slid myself on top of him and relieved him of his shirt. I kissed the crook of his neck as his hands fumbled to remove my shirt and bra. Once he had them off, I slid down his body and, with no great ceremony, I pulled down both his pants and underwear before engulfing his bulging member in my mouth. A gasp hissed from him as I took him in, sucking with deep, rough pulls. His hand found its way to my free one, and he thrust ever so slightly toward me, forcing me to take all of him in.

I came back off him and took my time tasting him, licking every inch. He moaned softly with my tender touches and I felt clenches deep within my own body with every sound that escaped his lovely lips. After an eternity, I slid my lips over him again, slowly taking his throbbing member into my mouth. A moan like a sigh flowed from him as I took it all in until my lips met where my fingers still caressed him. I rolled him in my mouth, moaning softly as I did my best to please him.

He soon pushed me off him and, sitting up, kissed me hungrily, seeking the wet warmth from our kisses. His free hand sought my breast and played with the nub, rubbing, squeezing, and pulling. My soft moans made him smile as his lips pulled away from mine and settled on my other nipple. My hands caressed his head as he licked me with his sandpaper tongue and his hand played with its twin. The lack of pain gave me the chance to focus on the pleasure and I moaned loudly, not even trying to soften my voice.

"Kisten..." I managed to squeeze out his name and

he paused, looking up to me. He panted loudly, his fangs visible and his eyes swirling with desire. Light spots were visible on his skin and I knew his animal was helping to drive his actions but, unlike last night, he was completely in control. They were on the same page about it this time, and I couldn't help my excitement.

"Yes?"

"Touch me here, please," I begged, moving his hand from my breast to my wet slit. He kissed the crook of my neck as he undid the snap at the front of my pants and slid a finger along my wet crease, rubbing against my swollen opening. I moaned for him again, my back arching as I finally felt him touch me without pain. The fire had distracted me from just how amazing it was to have him touch me and it was driving me insane.

"This is what you could have," Kisten purred, as he slowly slid two fingers inside and flexed them, watching my face as his actions served to increase my want. My whole body began to throb and pulse with my desire to have him inside me, to have him plunge his hardness into the depths that his fingers now searched. "What *we* could have."

He continued to tease me with his hand while kissing me, using both his fingers and tongue to mimic what he knew I wanted him to do with my body. Soon, my whole body was aflame with my desire for him and I tried to arch away from him, to pull away from his teasing hand and kiss. He wrapped his other arm around my middle, however, holding me where I was, forcing me to endure what I deemed torture. I wanted him inside me, and I knew he could tell; there was no way he couldn't smell how much I wanted him, how much I craved him.

Soon, he broke our kiss to steal a glimpse at my face, and I tried my best to glare, but I couldn't hold onto my annoyance. He smiled and nuzzled my chest and I moaned with frustration. Soon enough, he moved his hand away from my wet slit, and without the added distraction, I managed a halfhearted glare.

"You're being mean."

"I'm being dominant. I am still your Alpha, Raiven," Kisten growled, kissing my cheek as I turned away from him. "Don't worry. I'll give it to you soon enough."

I began to speak when he stood, picking me up and depositing me back on the bed. Swiftly, he removed our remaining clothing, leaving us both nude against the dark blue sheets. After undressing, he climbed on top of me and poised himself above my opening. However, instead of entering me as I wanted, he continued to tease me, only sweeping the outside.

"My, my, you are quite wet down here," I could hear the strain in his voice, knowing that he wanted to be inside me as much as I wanted him there, but couldn't resist the temptation to make me beg him. I began to squirm, and he had to hold me down, pinning my wrists to the bed. He grinned and leaned over me for a kiss, still teasing us both. Even as I kissed him back, I couldn't help my snide smile when we separated. "Feisty tonight."

"Well, if you would just fuck me already, I wouldn't have the energy to be feisty."

"True." He propped himself up and I was so wet,

he was able to thrust his full length inside me with one stroke. My hands dug into the sheets as my back arched, and I let out a loud moan as he filled me. Completely inside, Kisten took a moment, his entire body shaking as he enjoyed the sensation of finally being inside me. He leaned over me again, kissing my neck before whispering. "You okay?"

"I'm fine," I breathed, smiling up at him, my eyes half open. "How does it feel to finally give in to me?"

"Amazing." Kisten laughed low in his throat again, causing me to clench around him. Raising himself on his arms, he began to move inside me. The flames of passion that had danced in my lower regions now danced throughout my whole body and I couldn't remain still. I began to squirm as my hands searched for something, anything to hold on to, and soon Kisten had to hold me down again, pinning my wrists to the sheets once more.

"If you had wanted it this bad, you should have just told me." He shook his head and smiled, his eyes still swirling and his spots lightly appearing on his face. Somewhere amidst the thoughts that racked my mind and the heat and pleasure that racked my body, I found my voice.

"I believe I did a year ago, and you turned me down." I shot back and Kisten paused in his movements, leaning down to steal another painless kiss from my lips. I returned it as best I could, unable to help my moans as I raised my hips, trying to force the friction my body craved. The shifter's eyes had completely changed when he pulled away, his grin toothy as he smiled at me.

"Let me make up for that then." With that, he began to pound himself into me, and my hands freed themselves and found his shoulders. The pleasure was almost unbearable, and I felt as if I was drowning in it. Nothing else around us existed to me, except Kisten and the feel of him filling me. I was floating on a cloud of euphoria and pleasure, and he was the balloon that kept carrying me higher.

Moans I didn't recognize as my own and sounds I had never made before began to rise from me, faster and louder as he moved inside me. Kisten's growls grew in intensity as he leaned over me, and I could feel the sharp pain as he held my head with his clawed hand. I could feel the heat from his breath as he panted above me, and I moaned loudly as he bit my shoulder, his fangs penetrating deep.

For a moment, I wondered if I should try not to be so loud, lest someone heard us, but that moment passed, and I decided I didn't care if anyone heard me. The only thing that mattered was the heat and pleasure that resulted from having him inside me and my hands clenched the sheets as I orgasmed for what seemed like eternity. He began to pound himself into me harder and came inside me, whining softly as he released his seed. It was as if he wanted to fill me with his liquid heat and he gripped me tightly as he orgasmed.

Calming down, he gently pulled out and laid down beside me as I panted, still shaking from the residual pulses that my orgasms left in their wakes. Kisten was watching me with a smile, his fangs peeking out of his lips.

"Good enough?" Kisten asked between breaths, obviously tired, his form reverting to human. I merely moaned on the bed beside him, my body still shaking from fatigue. Kisten propped himself up, concerned about my lack of an answer. His hand touched my shoulder, and he looked at the blood with horror. "Raiven!"

"Fine," I managed to pant, giving him a quick thumbs-up as I focused on my breathing. Kisten jumped up from the bed, rushing into his bathroom so he could dress my wound. I hissed slightly as he squeezed the bite, trying to ensure that I would get no infection from his saliva. His movements were slow, as if he were worn out as well, but he dressed the bite properly, taping the gauze over the mark.

"Next time, say something, please." he whined, kissing my shoulder as he finished dressing the wound. I laughed slightly, raising my head to look at him. "You know my saliva is infectious."

"And miss out on that? Never." I blew him a kiss as he gave me an exasperated sigh. "Besides, I'll be all healed by morning from something like this."

"I know you'll heal, but it would not have been fun." He consented, placing the kit on his bedside table before laying a kiss on my stomach and resting his head against me. I closed my eyes, sighing happily as he stroked my thigh.

"I love you." His voice was soft when he spoke again and I sat up at this, forcing him to raise his head. My eyes met his and I reached for him, forcing him to slide back up the bed until we were face to face again. His eyes were shining, and he smiled at me softly as my eyes searched his. My heart pounded in my chest as I took in what he said, cradling his face in my hands. I couldn't help it as I laughed softly, gently kissing his sweet lips.

"I know," I smiled, my chest aching with how much I loved the man in my hands. Kisten purred, sliding us more onto the bed and under the sheets. He intertwined his legs with mine, clearly wanting to enjoy holding me for as long as he could. I buried my face into his chest, breathing him in happily as we settled in to sleep together.

16

I awoke alone in the bed and looked around to see Kisten standing in the doorway to his bathroom, his back to me. I watched him silently for a moment, taking in the view. He had evidently been up for a while; the bathroom mirror behind him was still foggy on the edges and his hair showed signs of dampness. He was fully dressed and engaged in the conversation, laughing quietly at something the other party said.

"...know that's not me." I heard him say, another soft laugh escaping him. From his words, I could only guess that the other person was Lucius, and it was likely they were talking about last night. I sat up slowly, stretching loudly as he turned around to look at me. He dropped his phone away from his ear and smiled at me, moving toward the bed. He covered the mouthpiece with his hand, leaning down to bury his face into my neck.

"Feel free to take a shower," he whispered, and the burning pain from the kiss he planted on my forehead reminded me of how much a blessing the previous night had been. I yawned, taking his suggestion as I slid out of the bed. Kisten hummed with contentment as I walked away and I turned around to find him enjoying the view. He had his phone back to his ear and silently blew me a kiss as I shook my head, stepping into the bathroom and closing the door behind me.

I turned on the shower and waited, looking at the bathroom mirror as I removed the bandage from my shoulder. The first thing I noticed was my hair and I frowned as I touched the glass. Using my power to challenge Lucius had caused my hair to grow quite a bit and I hated how my body reacted to my power. I pulled on one of the thick curls, deciding it wasn't worth cutting again yet. As I looked back to the mirror, I could see finger smudges in the glass and my curiosity grew as I looked at them. I breathed against the glass and revealed what was written: "I love you, Vogel[1]."

The words brought a wide smile to my face and I sighed happily as I tried to look at my back. The bite Kisten had given me had mostly healed, and I stepped into the shower slowly, waiting to see if the wound would hurt. The lack of pain was encouraging and I stepped fully into the running water.

As I basked under the warm water, letting it wash away my sleep, my thoughts returned to Aurel. I was still worried that he had seen me and Kisten in The Dream the night before, and I sighed heavily at the thought of having him confront me about it. It was all my fault and I accepted that: I should've told him the moment I realized that his feelings toward me had started to change. Kisten had always had my heart, but I knew how poorly Aurel reacted when he was rejected. He had already begun that process with me, and I just did not want to deal with it.

"Look at the mess you've made for yourself." I muttered under my breath, reaching to wash my body. I cleaned myself up and stepped out of the shower, seizing and wrapping a towel around my still dripping body. I walked back out into the bedroom to find it empty, with no sign of Kisten anywhere. A new outfit lay on the bed and I knew Kisten had not gone to my room to get my clothing. The red sundress that lay on the bed for me was nothing that I had ever owned, and I gingerly picked it up, unsure if I wanted to wear it.

"Still having doubts?" I heard Kisten's voice as he stepped back into the room, standing against the doorframe as I held the dress, turning to face him. His expression was hopeful but wary as he slowly stepped into the room, closing the door behind him. "I won't force you if you're not ready."

"What does wearing it mean?" I asked, and he smiled slightly, stepping closer to me. My heart pounded with his slow steps and I watched his every move until he stood directly in front of me.

"That I've chosen you," he stated, wrapping his arms around the towel as he held me close, pressing his face into my hair. He took a deep breath, releasing it shakily. "It tells others that I've decided to pursue you."

"How long have you had this?" I wondered aloud and Kisten chuckled, releasing me and stepping back to allow me to get dressed. I stood a moment longer, curious to hear his answer as I looked at the dress in my hands again. It wasn't common to see sundresses with sleeves and considering it didn't match any of the fall trends this year, I knew he had to have bought it before even asking me.

"Would you believe me if I said since I told you we couldn't keep seeing each other?" It was my turn to chuckle as I carefully laid the dress down and sat on the bed to slip on my underwear. Kisten merely watched me from where he stood, a smile glued to his face.

"So, your immediate reaction was to buy me a courting gift after telling me to go away?"

"Before. I bought it before," he admitted, looking down to the floor. I paused in my movements, surprised by his words. "I bought it on impulse, and that's when... when I knew I was falling too hard for you. That I would only end up hurting you more."

"I wish you had been honest, Kisten." I slipped on the dress, surprised by how well it fit me. I wasn't the type to wear dresses, so it was a little surprising that Kisten had been able to figure out my size. I spoke again as I slipped on the matching sandals he had provided, glancing around for a brush. "Good guess on the size, though. I'm impressed."

"I'm glad." The shifter handed me a hairbrush and I carefully tried to tame my longer curls, managing to brush them all out of my face. I knew they would spring forward again until I could properly style them, but at least they were out of my face for a while. As soon as I was done, Kisten wrapped his arms around me again, as if it pained him to keep his hands off me. I merely smiled up at him as he rocked me in his arms, smiling like an excited child at the sight of me wearing his dress. It warmed my heart to see him so happy and I carefully wrapped my arms around him, avoiding contact with his skin.

"So how exactly is this courting thing supposed to work?" I quizzed again, pulling back from the man holding me. Kisten grinned, holding his hand to his lips.

"Can't spoil all the fun. This is my first and only time doing this," he chirped, clearly pleased and excited. He motioned for me to follow him as he left the room. "Let me enjoy this."

"Fine, fine." I consented, following him and, closing his door quietly behind us, took a moment to look at his insignia. As expected, it had a leopard carved into the wood, with a large 'A' carved underneath. I assumed it stood for Alpha as I traced the shape, admiring the art as usual. I felt something cold and metallic drop around my neck and I looked down as Kisten placed a necklace on me, fastening it slightly above my locket. The necklace was a simple, gold 'R' and I turned to look at Kisten questioningly.

"Another courting thing?"

"Yes," he grinned, and it was clear he was enjoying this. "I was going to present it when I got home yesterday, but lost the chance with all the stuff going on with your case."

"So, this is what you wanted." I lifted it gently before I let it fall back against my skin. "What does this mean?"

"It shows that I've marked you as my future Beta and none of my pack can touch you or pursue you." Kisten beamed and I gave him a confused glance.

"Isn't that what the dress means?"

"In a way," he admitted, walking down the hall. I followed quietly behind him, waiting for him to finish. "The necklace is a specific sign to my pack: as long as you accept my courtship, you have to wear that at all times. The dress is just for today. Vampires also use red to mark pursuit, so everyone will know that you're mine."

Kisten whipped around quickly, wrapping his arms around me again as he pulled me into a deep kiss. I was again reminded of how nice the previous night had been as my lips and tongue ached with pain, but I forced myself to ignore it, doing my best to kiss him back. When he pulled back, his eyes were bright with a fire.

"It also shows that I've finally marked you." He whispered, his voice deep and sultry. I couldn't help but blush as he referenced the night before and he laughed darkly, releasing me. He motioned for me to continue following him and I found myself in the dining room. Sitting on the large table was a breakfast spread for one, and I knew immediately that this was what Kisten had left to prepare while I was showering.

"Is this another courting thing?" I groaned as I sat, Kisten pushing in my chair for me. He shook his head as he sat across from me, smiling brightly again.

"No, just me taking care of you," he chuckled, leaning on his hands to watch me. "I'm allowed to do something nice for you, aren't I?"

I didn't answer, merely blushing and turning my attention to the breakfast before me. Kisten had really gone out of his way, cooking me everything from waffles, to eggs, to bacon and sausage. He had even shaped the fruit to resemble flowers, making me almost not want to touch anything. Eventually, I began to eat and hummed with delight at the delicious food. After a few bites, I looked up to see Kisten still staring at me, his soft smile on his face. I lifted my arm as I coughed to hide my embarrassment, looking away again.

"What is it?"

"Nothing." He shrugged, never taking his eyes off me. I shifted uncomfortably under his gaze and Kisten chuckled softly again. "You are more easily embarrassed than one would think, huh?"

"It's been a while," I argued, taking another bite of food. Kisten leaned back in his chair, crossing his arms as he waited for me to continue. "I've never been courted before, but I haven't had even this kind of attention for a long time."

"Well, I'll make sure you get plenty of it." Kisten looked away as his phone went off again and he stood, excusing himself as he stepped out to take the call. Finally free of his staring, I focused on the delicious food he had prepared for me. I ate as much as I could and leaned back, quite full from the spread.

'You seem happy.' I heard my sister's voice rise in my mind and I sighed contently, closing my eyes in my chair.

"I am," I said aloud, glancing down at the remains of my breakfast. The flowered orange still sat untouched on its plate and I touched the fruit gingerly. "Kisten has a way of doing that."

'So, you've decided then? You chose to wear his dress.' I frowned at this, sitting up in my seat slightly. I heard my sister's exasperated sigh at my lack of an answer. *'Deny it all you want, but the fact you put it on shows where your intentions lie.'*

"I know, I just..." My voice trailed off and I didn't finish my sentence, my thoughts turning to my job, Eve and... Aurel. I shook my head, trying to focus on my determination. "I'm not going to run away, I want this too badly. It's just... it's gonna be complicated."

'*Guess you'll have to figure it out.*' My sister echoed Kisten's words as the man in question came back, hanging up his phone call. I was confused by the many phone calls as Kisten wasn't usually one to be on his phone much. Even if Lucius was the one he had been talking to earlier, the pair usually talked in person rather than making multiple phone calls. He looked at my mostly empty plates and smiled, removing the dishes from in front of me.

"Give me a moment to wash these and I'll get you to work." He promised, disappearing into the kitchen.

I smiled, closing my eyes again as I waited for Kisten to finish. I opened them again as the door opened, but it was not Kisten I found myself staring at. It was Aurel, who was giving my dress a strange look, eyeing me up and down with disbelief. His sea-green eyes were full of confusion and as they slowly drifted up to meet mine, I stood to explain.

"Aurel, I..."

"Who gave you that dress?" His voice sounded pained as he spoke, as if what he was seeing couldn't be real. The words got caught in my throat and I couldn't say anything as he stepped further into the room, causing me to step back from him. Aurel's expression changed from confusion to anger as he repeated his question. "Do you know what wearing a red dress means?"

"Yes, I—"

"She does." Kisten walked up behind me, sliding a white jacket onto my shoulders. I looked up to see his gaze and he was looking at Aurel, a smug smile on his face. I looked back to Aurel, who was waiting for me to deny it. When I said nothing, Aurel returned his eyes to Kisten, returning his dark glare. "I wouldn't have given it to her without explaining what it means."

"When did this happen?" Aurel sneered and the Alpha behind me chuckled, releasing my shoulders as he walked around the table to stand down the lich. I slowly slid on the provided jacket as Kisten smiled at Aurel, clearly enjoying flaunting this in his face. The lich turned his gaze to me, his eyes dark with jealousy. "Is this why you've been pushing me away?"

"Aurel..."

"No. This happened last night," Kisten interrupted me and Aurel kept his gaze on me, waiting for me to deny it. I shrugged, placing my hands on the back of the chair as I met his gaze evenly. Kisten laughed at his reaction, earning himself a hiss from the lich. "She's wearing the dress, isn't she, Aurel? What more proof do you need?"

"You tricked her." Aurel hissed, clearly not wanting to believe what Kisten was saying. I quickly released the chair, shocked by the lich's words. Kisten shrugged, his grin broadening as Aurel continued. "Raiven wouldn't choose you. She wouldn't lock herself to one person."

"If that's what you want to believe." With this, he turned to me, motioning for me to come to him. "C'mon, Raiven, I need to get you to work."

I carefully walked around the table as Kisten held the door for me, and I kept my gaze from meeting Aurel's as I followed him out of the dining room. Once the door had closed behind us, I took a moment to breathe a sigh of relief. I glanced up to see Kisten looking at me, his dark smile still on his face.

"How was that for him finding out?" He asked innocently and I looked away, still torn about the whole confrontation. I realized that Kisten had probably set Aurel up to see me in the dress, especially after finding out he wanted me for his harem. I started walking away, muttering under my breath.

"Probably as bad as if he had seen us in the club last night."

Kisten chuckled at this, wrapping his arm around my waist as he caught up to me. He took a moment to breathe me in before leading me down the hall, heading for the surface.

"Maybe, but I think I like this better." Kisten leaned to plant a kiss in my hair, never pausing in his stride. I was tempted to look over my shoulder, but decided against it, not wanting to see Aurel behind me. Kisten must have noticed, as he glanced back and waved to someone behind us. From his deep chuckle, I could guess who it was as he whispered into my ear. "Hard to think we were once friends."

"Friends?" I repeated, and Kisten nodded, his dark look fading for a moment to a softer expression.

"Aurel... Well, he never seemed to be bothered by my distant behavior. Eventually, he reached out to me, saying it looked like I could use a friend." Kisten's expression returned to its dark glare and his smile was full of anger. "Turns out he just wanted me for his harem and was trying to butter me up first. As you can guess, I didn't take finding out any better than he took my refusal."

"Sounds familiar," I muttered, thinking of Aurel's words in the dining room. I didn't want to believe that the lich had only befriended me to seduce me, but I couldn't deny the possibility, especially with the

181

way he had handled me choosing someone else. Kisten squeezed my waist, encouraging me to continue. "I mean, Aurel was the one who sought me out to be friends."

"Sounds like him. I'm glad you chose me instead." Kisten released me as we climbed up the stairs and I stepped into the afternoon sun. I saw that his car was now in the parking lot and looked at him questioningly. Kisten shrugged, pulling out his keys from his pocket. "I woke up this morning. You're the one who slept most of the day."

"Gee, I wonder why," I remarked sarcastically and he laughed, kissing my hair as he walked past me. I glanced at my car, still sitting in her parking spot. "You know my car is here, I can drive myself."

"Of course you can." Kisten smiled, leaning over his open door as I went to my car to retrieve my phone. I had no missed messages, meaning last night had gone smoothly without our suspect showing up. "But I enjoy having you in mine and I'm doing you a favor by saving your gas."

I couldn't help but smile as I closed my door and stepped into the passenger side of his car. As we pulled away, I noticed Aurel standing on the sidewalk outside the Coven. Our eyes locked for a moment and my thoughts turned to what Kisten had said about Aurel's intentions. As we drove away, I couldn't help but worry about the mess I had gotten myself into.

17

I leaned against the glass terrarium, sipping my drink and adjusting my dark sunglasses as the groups of people walked by me. As soon as we had reached the office, Brandon had shooed me right back out; he wanted me to take Julia's place at the Landing, watching for our culprit. She had stayed at The Dream all night with Aurel and was asleep at her house to get ready to do it again. We didn't want to risk him at the Landing without us having eyes there, so I was Brandon's next pick.

We were the only two women on the team and he was hoping we could act as bait for our witch, getting him to approach us of his own accord. This unfortunately would've meant I had to work with Aurel, but a quick call on Kisten's part saved me from my fate. I smoothed my dress, finishing off my beverage and tossing it into the trash next to me.

"Ready to move somewhere else?" Kisten came up behind me and I turned to look at him. He was wearing a dark red button-up shirt and khaki pants, as well as matching shades to mine. A fancy watch finished off his look and he easily blended in with the usual high-class shoppers that frequented the Landing. I was still wearing the red sundress and white jacket, with the added trappings of a red purse and some gold bangles around my wrists. I was uncomfortable with so much extra baggage, but both Kisten and Brandon had insisted it would allow me to blend in better. I glanced at my phone, noting the time before shrugging.

"I guess, let's shift a little closer to The Dream." I stood up and started walking off in front of him, pretending to be interested in the various store fronts. Kisten walked behind me, glancing for anyone following us. He moved a little closer to me, leaning down to whisper in my ear.

"Wouldn't you blend in better if you actually looked like you were shopping?" he offered, and I turned to see the devilish grin on his face. Even with the sunglasses hiding his eyes, I knew his intentions were far from just helping me blend in. I shrugged him off as I kept walking.

"Not really the shopping type."

"C'mon, it'll help you blend in." Kisten stopped my stride and turned me towards a lingerie store. My cheeks burned with embarrassment as I pulled away from him and I could hear him chuckling behind me.

"I guess I could try." I stepped into a clothing store near The Dream and pretended to be interested in the various items of women's clothing. I turned around to see Kisten sitting outside, relaxing on the bench across from the store. I rolled my eyes as I returned to my window shopping, lifting a green halter that was much too short for my tastes.

"Do you need some help, ma'am?" I turned to look as one of the shopkeepers approached me, her fake smile beaming as she waited for my answer. I politely smiled back and shook my head, watching as the harpy fluffed her wings.

"No thank you, just looking."

"Well, let me know if you need anything... else..." Her voice trailed off as she looked me up and down, as if finally noticing my dress. Her eyes worked their way up to the necklace and she glanced outside to Kisten, her eyes widening. Her voice was low and shaking when she spoke again. "You're with the Alpha? A-Are you sure you don't need any help? I can help you find whatever you need. We have the latest in holo-rooms, you can try on whatever you would like..."

"I'm fine, sweetie." I tried to smile, starting to wish I hadn't worn the dress. I hadn't expected to run into anyone from the pack and I was still embarrassed by its implied meaning. The girl seemed worried and she glanced back towards Kisten and I followed her gaze. I couldn't tell if he was looking at us or not due to the sunglasses, but just knowing he was there was enough to frazzle the girl, as if we were testing her. I gently laid my hand on her feathers and she jumped under my touch.

"Hey, sweetie," I started, and she looked up at me sheepishly. I forced myself to smile brightly as I lifted my sunglasses, looking at her face-to-face. "No need to get worked up, I'm simply browsing. I'm not really looking to buy anything here. Kisten's not here to judge you or anything."

"Thank goodness." She was relieved as she walked away and I continued my walk through the aisle, not really finding anything that interested me. I eventually found myself in the aisle containing jewelry and I paused for a moment, taking in the latest trends. I was about to walk away when one of the rings caught my eye and I gently lifted it to get a better look.

It was a replica of one of my rings, although clearly costume jewelry and a poor imitation of the real thing. After escaping from Mater Vitae's Hunters, I had lost the ring before recently reclaiming it from a collector. The man had been proud to flaunt it, as virgin rainbow opals were extremely rare and until discovering my ring, most believed that there was only one in the world. Since my ring held the second known stone, the man had been reluctant to part with it before I persuaded him it wasn't worth his life. It didn't surprise me that it would still be in the public consciousness, considering its rarity and recent spotlight.

"*Arcus Pluvius.*" I read the tag aloud, a name the public had given it. My memories drifted back to the one who had given it to me, during a time long forgotten by most. It had been a parting gift, a reminder that they had once existed before Mater Vitae erased them. They had already known that she would not forgive them for their trespass, no matter how special they were. Mother was always creating new species back then and killed off any if they caused her too much trouble. Mother never had an issue using her Hunters to kill off one of her mistakes, but they had been different, and she did the deed herself.

We were both singular successes that she had not been able to replicate and thus we were kept in the equivalents of birdcages: able to be looked upon and appreciated for the rarities we were, but never free. I was probably one of the few alive who remembered them, and it had been their death that had given me the nerve to try to escape. Shortly after, the First also rebelled, so it was easy to say that it was their execution that had started everything and led to Mater Vitae retreating to wherever she now was.

"Remembering something?" I dropped the ring in surprise and turned to Kisten who was standing behind me. He slowly bent to pick up the ring from the floor, examining it as he stood. I watched him, wondering if he recognized it. After a while he shrugged, looking at me. "Pretty, for a fake."

"I have the real one." I whispered, watching him place it back. Kisten raised his eyebrows as I met his gaze through the sunglasses.

"Wait...isn't that the ring some big shot collector bought at an auction a couple of years ago?" he wondered, and I nodded, beginning to make my way through the store. "I remember Lucius telling me it belonged to a member of Mater Vitae's court before she killed them. No one had known what happened to the ring until it showed up at the auction."

"It was given to me, right before they were killed. I had always managed to hold onto it, but finally lost it when I crossed the sea. I was surprised when it turned up at the auction." I sighed, weaving my way back through the clothing. "And the collector was difficult to convince, but I wasn't leaving without it. It had been a gift, a way to remember them."

"You knew the Seraph?" Kisten asked and I nodded, stepping out of the store back into the bright sunlight. I looked up to the blue sky with its soft clouds and smiled wistfully.

"We were similar in our uniqueness and Mother had our rooms close enough together that we sometimes got the chance to talk." I spoke quietly, watching the fluffy clouds as they rolled by. Kisten stood next to me, also looking up. "They were the closest thing I had to a friend in those times. I think they felt the same way, since they gave me the ring."

"What did they do?" Kisten asked quietly and I shifted my gaze to him, slightly surprised. "To be executed?"

"You don't know?"

"I only know what Lucius told me when we left Europe, which is very little." Kisten shrugged, glancing down at me. "I was only about fifty years old when I agreed to come with him, and he has never really been talkative about his time with Mother. The most he told me was it was the Seraph's death and your escape that convinced him and the others that they needed to leave too."

"He revealed a flaw in her system. We both always knew that her blood didn't bind us the same way, but we had been careful to avoid allowing her to find out," I admitted, looking back up to the sky. "They disobeyed her command, to save someone else from her wrath. Once she realized she couldn't control them, she killed them. I was sure I would be next, so I found the courage to leave."

'More like I kicked your ass, but whatever.' My sister rose to make her snide remark, but Kisten interrupted me before I could rebuke her.

"I assume the First rebelled for similar reasons?"

"I'm not sure." I sighed, closing my eyes and turning away from the sky. My thoughts turned to Nisaba, and how she was the one who allowed me to escape that fateful night. "I never really knew any of the First personally, just their names. If I had to guess,

I would imagine that they finally had enough of her and, after finding out I had managed to escape, figured they could do the same."

"And that's how she lost control?" He asked quietly and I nodded again.

"Yeah, the First began to offer protection to those who didn't want anything to do with her, creating the Overseer system." I drew a deep breath, remembering the turmoil that had followed. The Dark Ages had been a time of darkness and madness for those of us who lived in the shadow of humans. "She sent her Hunters after all of us, but as members of the First were killed, other Supes realized they could offer the same protection as Overseers. As the idea spread and more and more Overseers appeared, I think she finally accepted she couldn't regain control through force and disappeared. Hunters still chase after me and any First who remain, but this is a far better life than the one I had."

Kisten said nothing to this, following me silently as I weaved through the sea of shoppers and people. I had never dreamed I would have such freedom while I was in Mater Vitae's court and certainly never thought I would've survived as long as I did. Her Hunters were always searching and never seemed far from my trail, no matter how well I tried to hide it. The fact I hadn't encountered any in the past three years was already a blessing, but I had accepted that there would come a day when I lost this millennia-old struggle.

But not today. I thought, turning to Kisten behind me, who paused as I turned to face him. I studied him for a moment before smiling, and he slowly returned my smile. Stepping up to me, he lifted his sunglasses

KIRRO BURROWS

as he leaned down to kiss me and I leaned up to him, despite the searing pain. He smiled softly at me with his chartreuse eyes before dropping the sunglasses back down and walking past me. I couldn't help my stupid grin as I followed, sighing with happiness.

18

I stood amongst the busy people as Kisten stepped into a store, insisting that he would buy me "something appropriate" for blending in with the other shoppers. I started to argue that plenty of people came to the Landing to window shop, but he was having none of it, disappearing into another women's clothing store. I shook my head as I sighed, unable to help my smile. It was nice to spend time with Kisten like this again, and I hummed as I adjusted the bangles on my wrists.

I began to glance around the growing crowd, ever watchful to catch our suspect. However, I was soon distracted by the number of couples walking around together, arm in arm, hanging all over the other. My heart ached slightly, but a smile soon grew on my face despite the discomfort. I no longer had a reason to be envious of others; it was merely a matter of time before Kisten and I could be the same.

"Raiven?" I instantly froze as I heard the voice behind me and I swallowed hard, refusing to turn around. I could hear his footsteps as he drew closer and I knew that he would not be so easy to get rid of. "Raiven, look at me."

"What, Aurel?" I turned to face the lich, crossing my arms as I did so. His orange curls bounced, and his eyes still held hints of his anger and disbelief. I was glad for my sunglasses, hiding the uncertainty in my eyes while I did my best to speak with confidence. "Shouldn't you be resting for tonight with Julia?"

"Why?" he begged, and if not for the anger that was hidden in his expression, I might have believed his distress was real. I shook my head, frustrated with myself: I should have been able to read through his intentions sooner. Aurel placed his hands on my arms, gripping me tightly. "Why him? You... you're not like that."

"Because I love him." I breathed, breaking free of Aurel's grip as I stepped away from him. My actions had caught some attention, but most people kept walking as if they didn't notice. I glanced around quickly before returning my eyes to Aurel. "He's been my choice since I came here, Aurel. Justina was the only other person I wanted and, well... she's taken."

"He's still bound by the Oath of Loyalty. You can't have him either," Aurel pointed out and I shrugged, doing my best to pretend it didn't bother me. "He's just binding you into a one-sided relationship. You know that."

"Lucius gave him a night free of the Oath to pursue me, so honestly, I'm not all that worried that he won't free him entirely. Evalyn may not want to, but she's not the Overseer." My calm tone hid my inner turmoil and for a moment, I was assured in my relationship with Kisten. The confidence was infectious, and I couldn't help my smug smile as I continued. "I didn't have to wear this dress, Aurel, Kisten didn't force me. I *chose* to because I love him."

"He is tricking you." Aurel hissed, still trying to convince me to side with him. I laughed, finally removing my sunglasses from my face as I gave him an incredulous look.

"Tricking me? Kisten has been nothing but honest with me, even when he pushed me away. If he wanted to 'trick' me so badly, then why keep me at arm's length for more than a year?" I glared at Aurel, refusing to look away from his gaze. "I'm not so sure you can say the same. Kisten told me about your pursuit of him, how you pretended to want to be friends in order to lure him into your harem."

"I have never lied to you, Raiven. I did want to be friends with you, and eventually I wanted more than that. I thought you wanted the same." He insisted, stepping closer to me as I stepped back again. My demeanor cracked for a moment with his plea and he immediately moved to take advantage of it. "I admit what I did with Kisten was wrong, but that was long before I met you. Please, Raiven, reconsid—"

"No," I stated plainly, not letting him finish the thought. I wanted to slap myself for being so stupid. I had valued having a friend so much that I had overlooked the obvious. Aurel was obsessed with his collections, be it jewelry or people and while he treated his collections well, he was relentless when he wanted to add to them. Just as he had begged me for my jewelry, he was refusing to let me slip away from him. "I have made my choice. I made it long before I put on this dress."

"Raiven—"

"Something wrong, *mein Liebling*[1]?" Kisten came

193

up behind me, placing his hand on my shoulder as he leaned around to hand me my shopping bag. It felt heavy as I accepted it and I glanced inside to see it full of various outfits. I looked up at Kisten, who shrugged as he shifted his attention to Aurel, his dark smile returning. "Ah, come to beg some more? I think she's given you her answer."

"Fuck off, Kisten." Aurel hissed, dropping his desperate act for pure anger. Kisten chuckled low in his throat, gripping my shoulder tightly. I was worried for a moment that he was losing control as his hands began digging into my shoulder, hints of his claws stabbing my skin. I looked up at his face, but his expression was calm, only his burning eyes revealing his emotions.

"Or what? I'm the Alpha, Aurel. You can't do anything to me *or* her," Kisten gloated, brushing his hand across my hair before planting a soft kiss. Aurel growled and the semi-interested crowd was now extremely interested, many people stopping to watch the display. I began to feel uncomfortable under their gaze, but Kisten shifted his hand from my shoulder to my waist, keeping me pinned to his side. "I think you should just leave us alone before you get in trouble again."

Again?

"You turned me down, Kisten. I don't like it but I can accept that," Aurel said, not trying to appeal to anyone's emotions anymore. He had his eyes locked on me, his pupils boring into me as he spoke. "But you don't have the right to take her from me. She won't be happy trapped in a relationship with you."

"I believe she told you the truth, Aurel. She chose me long before you decided you needed another 'rare beauty' for your harem." Kisten hissed, no longer trying to hide his anger or jealousy, either. It was starting to seem more like a personal vendetta than fighting over me and I squirmed in Kisten's arms. "Maybe you should learn to accept that not everyone wants you."

"Aurel, *please*," I begged, cutting the lich off before he could speak. His eyes continued to stare into my soul and I sighed heavily before continuing. "I should've said something about me and Kisten before now. Blame me for that if you want, but all of this is unnecessary. I told you yesterday; I have never felt more than friendship for you and I never wanted more."

"Hearts can change easily." Aurel spat, looking up to meet Kisten's gaze as he snarled.

The Alpha smiled, releasing me as he walked up to Aurel, once again using his superior height to stare him down. The crowd was now whispering, and I knew there had to be those present who recognized who we were. All Supernaturals in The Capital had a vague idea of who was a part of the Coven, and many of those in Decver were definitely capable of recognizing us on sight. I clutched the shopping bag with both hands as I tried to ignore the burning stares.

"You're right, Aurel." Kisten's voice was dripping with sarcasm and jealousy as he spoke, his dark smile widening. "But I guess you'll just have to wait and see. Because right now..."

Kisten leaned down into the lich's face, almost close enough to kiss him. He whispered quietly into Aurel's ear and even though I couldn't hear what he was saying, I knew the words he was baiting him with.

"She's mine, and I won't give her up easily." With this, Kisten patted Aurel's shoulder and began to walk away. The gawkers began to awkwardly disperse, and Kisten turned to look at me where I stood. I understood his silent question and, glancing back at Aurel one final time, I slid on my sunglasses as I jogged up to him. The lich was standing still, his eyes still locked on Kisten's back.

"Just doesn't know when to quit, huh?" Kisten breathed, reaching to take my hand in his. I was surprised by the lack of pain and I looked down to notice that he had slipped on a leather glove, protecting me from the pain of this simple gesture. I looked back up to see a soft smile on his face and he lifted my hand to kiss it.

"I don't want to hurt you every time." Kisten whispered, dropping our hands as we continued walking. I giggled softly, squeezing his hand in mine as he continued. "Sorry about Aurel, by the way. He's unlikely to give up for a while, given his persistence in the past."

"Because of you?" I offered and then I dropped my voice, uncertainty filling me. "Or because of me?"

"I mean, we both know Aurel has never taken rejection well." Kisten shrugged, glancing at the other stores we walked past. His eyes lingered on The Dream for a moment, but he led us past, not stopping. "But I'm sure he thinks I'm trying to get revenge for what he did by taking you. And he's not completely wrong, just has things in the wrong order."

"You didn't even know about that until last night," I argued and Kisten shrugged again, his face showing his annoyance. It took me a moment to realize what he had fully said and I looked at him with surprise. "Wait. What do you mean by wrong order?"

"Why do you think I took you to The Dream, knowing Aurel would be there?" Kisten chuckled low in his throat, squeezing my hand tightly. "I almost didn't answer his call last night but I had wanted to rub you in his face. Finding out about Irida distracted me, but never changed my intention. Finding out he wanted you, well, that just made it that much better."

"Rub me in his face?" I asked darkly and Kisten looked down at me and, seeing my dark look, kissed my forehead gently. I stopped walking and he turned to face me, his loving smile back on his face. "I thought you didn't know about Aurel and me."

"I didn't, not until you told me. I just wanted to show him *I* had moved on." Kisten sighed happily as he looked at me. My anger started to melt away under his loving gaze and he pulled me close as he finished. "I'll spare you the details, but Aurel insisted no one else would be willing to put up with me. I wanted to rub it in his face that someone would. He would've hated seeing me with anyone, but because of you, someone who also doesn't want him...

"Well, let's just say he—" Kisten stopped speaking as he looked up, seeing Aurel walking up to us quickly. The lich's feet barely touched the ground and he was half-flying as he moved toward us. Kisten glanced around and his eyes rested on the bathrooms. He gently pushed me in their direction, and I turned to give him a confused look.

"He's not going to give up and I don't want you to be at the center of it again. This is more about us than you at this point." He smiled and I reluctantly went, looking back as Aurel reached Kisten. He looked as if he was going to strike him, but Kisten merely smiled, not remotely intimidated by the lich's aggression. I walked inside, disappearing before Aurel could notice.

I didn't need to use the toilet, so I merely took my sunglasses off and splashed some water on my face at the sink. I closed my eyes, grimacing at the thoughts that were rising up about Aurel and doing my best to push past them. I took a deep breath and let it out shakily as I began to open my eyes.

"This *courting* thing is really becoming a mess," I said out loud, frowning as I looked at my reflection. My thoughts returned to the girl's reaction in the clothing store and I carefully lifted the necklace Kisten had given me. I was still confused by her worry and fear, and wondered if the necklace meant more than just 'marking me'. Kisten wasn't the type to lie outright, but he was the type to omit information at times. I resolved to ask him as I dropped the necklace, turning to retrieve my bag from the floor.

A gloved hand appeared over my mouth and I immediately moved to retaliate until I felt a knife placed against my chest. I turned my eyes to see our suspect behind me, his dark brown eyes twisted with malice and his matted black hair peeking out from underneath his hood. He was still wearing the same outfit from Thursday night and he scowled at me in the mirror.

"Your Overseer has my Irida." He hissed, pressing the knife into my skin. The knife was silver and he was aiming for my heart, so I knew he had taken me to be a shapeshifter. As I was walking around with the Alpha, it was a reasonable assumption for him to make and I remained still, trying to think of my next move. While the silver itself was not a heavy concern, the knife was and I didn't want to risk him getting away if I defended myself, especially not with him so close.

"What do you want?" I breathed, doing my best to sound scared and worried. He pressed the knife deeper into my skin as he spoke again, the tip drawing a thin line of blood.

"I'm going to take you with me," he snarled, pulling us backwards towards a stall. "I've already left your Alpha a little present, letting him know I have his mate. Unless he brings me my Irida, I will kill you."

I gasped as we started to sink into the floor, failing to realize that he had drawn a Circle into the tiles. The door burst open and I saw Kisten and Aurel rush into the bathroom, not worried about what others thought. I reached up to my chest, tearing the locket housing my sister's soul from around my neck. I tossed it to Kisten before I disappeared completely into the bathroom floor and blacked out in the darkness.

19

When I came to, I was in a dark, dirty cage and surrounded by trees. I groaned as I sat up, trying to see if the witch was anywhere nearby. I couldn't see any signs of him in the darkness, so I tested the bars of my cage.

They were silver, as I expected, and a small test with my power proved that I could easily bend them. The culprit was so sure I was a shapeshifter, he didn't even bother to ensure the cage was sturdy, certain the silver would keep me from trying. Not wanting to give up my advantage, I left the bars alone and looked around the small clearing I was being kept in.

It was evident that he had been staying here for a short while, probably since Irida stopped herself from killing Justina. He knew it was a matter of time before we would be looking for him, so he was at least smart enough not to remain in the city. He had a small cooler and chair, with a dirty sleeping bag next to an equally dirty backpack. I couldn't see anything around me but trees, so I had no indication how far we were from the city or what direction the city would be in. There was barely any sunlight left in the sky above me, and from the drop in temperature, I knew it had been at least a few hours since he had taken me from the bathroom.

"You're awake," I turned around as the witch appeared from the darkness of the woods, and he dropped to his haunches near the cage, glaring at me. I glared back, not even pretending to be afraid. He scoffed at this, producing a gun and he showed me the silver bullets in his other hand before loading it. "Behave."

I merely hissed at this as he walked away, watching him as he moved about his camp, retrieving something to drink from his cooler. He plopped down in his chair while downing the beverage, tossing the aluminum can into the trees near my cage. I saw it was alcohol and rolled my eyes, annoyed by this man's arrogance as he drank a second one. He clearly was too full of himself if he thought capturing me would get him what he wanted. Even if I had been Evalyn, no one was going to hand Irida to him: the only thing he was getting from anyone was a decent helping of death.

"Hmmmm," I looked up as the witch hummed and I nearly gagged from the look in his eyes. He was rubbing himself with the gun, and I knew what he was imagining. I growled at him, allowing my eyes to swirl with power before turning away. All I had to do was keep him near me long enough for Kisten and my team to find me, then everything would be over for him. My locket would lead them straight to me, as my sister could only survive if the locket was near my heart and it was designed to find its way back to me.

"You're prettier than that stupid bitch." I glared at him as he mentioned Justina and he smiled at my reaction, grabbing himself with his hand. "She should've just accepted the threesome with me and Irida and she never would've been hurt. Now I have to kill them both: a waste if you ask me, it'll be hard to find someone as easy to control as Irida."

"*You* are fucking disgusting." I spat and he stood up, overturning his chair and dropping the gun in his anger. He stomped towards me and reached through the bars, wrapping his hand around my throat. I instinctively reached to grab his wrist, but I realized there was no power in his grip. I chuckled, giving him a look of pity as I dropped my hand. "You're so fucking weak. Now I understand why Irida thought you were human. You have to control someone else to pull off a kill because there's no way you could ever dream of hurting someone."

"Shut up, bitch!" He snarled, tightening his grip – but for a Supernatural, it was a joke. I easily pushed his hand from around my neck and sat comfortably in my cage. He seemed ready to reach for me again, but instead, he stood and went back to his overturned chair. He retrieved the gun and released the safety, shooting me in the cage. I gasped with pain as the bullet went through my left arm, and I held my hand to the wound as the red began to stain my white jacket. He laughed with triumph as he came back up to the cage and pointed the gun towards my head.

"Now, it is a matter of time before the silver kills you." He laughed, leaning close to my cage. "Hope your boyfriend is quick on his feet, I'd hate to have to try and steal someone else."

"You won't leave this forest alive." I swore and yelped with pain as he shot me again, this time catching my midsection. I was tempted to free myself from the cage and stomp him into the ground, but his shots were purposely missing anywhere vital. He was counting on the silver slowly killing me, which ironically would be his undoing. Despite having the abilities of vampires, I was much easier to kill thanks to still being somewhat human, and major trauma to my heart or brain would easily render me lifeless. The silver would only slow my healing, so as long as he avoided a kill shot, I knew I would recover from these injuries.

I forced myself to act as if my body was racked with pain as he gloated over me, pleased with my reaction. He looked at the gun with a savage grin and for a moment, I thought he was going to shoot me again for fun. It was obvious from his behavior that he had never thought of using one before, which wasn't surprising. Most Supernaturals preferred their own abilities over human weapons and it was seen as a weakness to rely on them. He placed the gun on the ground before he crouched in front of the cage again.

"Maybe I should have my fun with you before you die," he grabbed my chin, pulling my face closer to his. I spat in his face and it was his turn to growl as he backed away from me again. He wiped my saliva from his face, then he grinned at me, clearly liking this new idea. He carefully picked up the gun again and put it in my face. I was forced to comply as he pulled me out of the cage and stepped on my back, the gun still to my head. "Ruin you as a potential mate."

The witch started to slowly lift the back of my jacket and I began to summon my power as he stroked my back with his free hand. He would kill me if he pulled the trigger, but there was no way I was going to let this sleaze have his way with me. The ground around us began to shake and heave as my power grew and he paused, looking at the shifting dirt around us. Not seeing any reason for the tremor, he instantly connected the dots and he pressed the gun harder into my head, forcing my face into the ground.

"Stop it," he hissed, and I flinched as he fired the gun next to my head. He leaned over me, shoving his foot more firmly into my back. The pain in my side increased from the added pressure and the blood began to flow more quickly as he spoke directly into my ear. "I don't care what you are, a silver bullet through your skull and heart will end you."

I hissed, but withdrew my power, the ground becoming still once again. The witch smiled above me, and he once again began to touch me with his free hand, taking his foot off my back. I clenched my teeth in the dirt, wanting nothing more than to throw this sorry excuse for a person off my back. There was a small chance I could move faster than he could pull the trigger, but I knew there was no way I could dodge the bullet entirely.

I reached my boiling over point when the man's hand slid down to my posterior and I growled as he took his time fondling me, gripping and groping me through the dress. When he started to slide his hand between my legs, I decided to make my move, not willing to let this man touch me anymore. I moved my hands underneath my chest and, ignoring the bullet hole in my arm, began to prop myself up. He pushed the gun into my skull more but, upon noticing that he couldn't force me back to the ground, I heard him begin to pull the trigger.

Moving as fast as I could, I bucked my back and

rolled away from the witch as my head exploded with pain. I was slower than usual, as my previous wounds were slowing me down and I held my head as I began to bleed from the gunshot wound. The man stood, aiming the gun at me again, but he was distracted by a tremendous noise approaching us. A large blur shot from the trees behind him and pinned him to the ground, my locket in its mouth. The gun went off as it flew from his hand as he was forced into the dirt and Kisten placed his large paw on the witch's head, growling loudly. The rest of my team followed behind him, with Lucius and Aurel also stepping into the space, the Overseer's presence alone intimidating in the growing darkness. As Brandon placed the barrel of his gun on the man's head, Kisten got off him, padding his way to me as he shifted.

"Raiven," his voice was full of relief which then turned to worry as he noticed the blood flowing between my fingers where I held my head. He was still wearing his red shirt and khakis and I smiled slightly at seeing him. Kisten ignored my smile and turned to call over his shoulder. "Justin, over here, now!"

Justin moved from behind Brandon to Kisten's side, revealing the Alpha's trauma kit as he holstered his gun. Kneeling in front of me, Justin removed my jacket and began to address the wound to my arm as Kisten gingerly touched my side, ripping my dress to examine the wound there. He returned his attention to my face after instructing Justin how to temporarily dress the bullet hole and he laid his hand on mine, gently moving it away from my head. I closed my eyes as he examined the damage, the first tingles of light-headedness hitting me. The bullet had grazed the side of my head, taking off the top of my right ear and Kisten growled as he moved to dress the wound.

"Kis..." I tried to whisper his name, but now that my adrenaline was fading, I suddenly found myself weak and struggling to speak. Kisten quickly hushed me, placing my locket in my hand. I immediately felt my sister's concern and her voice burst into my mind as soon as I closed my fingers over the wood.

'Raiven, you idiot! What were you thinking, allowing yourself to be bait? This bullshit isn't worth your life, dammit!' She screamed, and I groaned, as her yelling was making my headache even worse. *'You should've killed that excuse for a witch the minute he touched you!'*

'Better me than Julia, and if I hadn't allowed him to take me, he would've just run. We might have never caught him,' I reasoned, closing my eyes as I answered her. Kisten must've worried that I was passing out as he gently shook me. He sighed with relief when I opened my eyes, and I smiled softly at him again. I could still feel my sister's frustration and relief, but she didn't continue, instead fading away. I knew she was saving her words for later, once I was in a safer place.

"Can you stand?" Kisten's voice was soft and tender as he stood me up and I wobbled on my feet, dizzy from the blood loss. I fell into his arms and he scooped me up, careful to avoid putting unnecessary pressure on my wounded side and arm. Kisten adjusted me in his arms and turned as Brandon finished speaking to the witch.

"... sure the other Overseers would love a chance to punish you for your crimes and usually we'd pass you off to the first one you pissed off. But as you're in my jurisdiction now and harmed a member of my team..." Brandon looked up to Lucius and the Overseer nodded. My boss's face turned savage as Julia pulled the man to his knees, keeping their guns pointed at him. The man hissed at Julia touching him, but she merely shoved her gun harder into his back.

Lucius stepped up to the witch, who, despite obviously being overwhelmed, looked into the vampire's eyes defiantly.

"Fuck you!" He spat on the ground in front of Lucius, but the Overseer barely noticed: his eyes were locked on the sorry excuse for a man before him. The witch spat again, clearly aiming for Lucius' clothing. "You all think you're so much better than me just because you have longer fucking lives."

"*No.*" Lucius' voice boomed through the trees, even though it was barely above a whisper. I heard the birds scatter into the night sky and other creatures scattered as well, sensing the killing intent in the air. "The woman you harmed and the woman you used won't even live as long as you. I'm not better than you because I've lived longer."

"Lamias are good for controlling, weak minds and weak hearts," the witch gloated, clearly feeling no remorse for what he had done to Irida. "As for that other bitch, sorcerers are better off dead anyway."

"You are disgusting," Aurel offered, speaking in Lucius' place. The lich walked up to the man and very cleanly sliced off the man's left arm with his newly shifted claws. I narrowed my eyes as the man screamed, gripping his new stump as his blood poured out. Aurel grinned savagely: due to his body-based magic, Lucius often gave Aurel the honor of doling out punishment to those who deserved it.

Aurel licked the blood from his hand, his eyes aglow with excitement. "You will suffer for your crimes."

The man didn't respond, staring at his missing arm with horror and anguish. He looked up and with anger in his eyes, spat in Lucius' direction again, finally reaching the vampire's shoes. At this, Lucius reacted, reaching down and lifting the man into the air by his throat, the vampire's feet hovering above the ground. My team and Aurel stepped back as the air was flooded with electricity, small flashes of lightning visible from the sudden change in charge. The man finally seemed to understand his position as he squirmed in the Overseer's grip, trying to free himself from Lucius.

"You, are simply trash." I buried my face in Kisten's chest as I felt the intense electricity in the air, and I knew Lucius had fried the witch as I heard the corpse hit the ground. Lucius was rarely so violent, usually locking up anyone we caught into the Basement or giving the honor of execution to Aurel, but as the witch was a being without remorse, I understood why Lucius had wanted to do it himself. It wasn't as if we could follow Division 11 protocol, either: even without a proper wand, his ability to control others made him too dangerous to attempt transport and it would've been equally dangerous to try to hold him for another Overseer to arrive.

Kisten watched calmly, only looking down to make sure I was still awake. His expression was as stoic as Lucius' had been and I wanted to reach up to touch his face, but lacked the strength to try. I instead closed my eyes, burying my face against him again as he carried me out of the woods, and into the waiting transport. I chanced a glance as we walked by Aurel, but the lich's expression was unreadable as we passed him.

Kisten placed me on the waiting gurney and climbed into the back of the ambulance beside me. He immediately started prepping my IV and I found the strength to move, using my free hand to touch his leg. He paused in his movements, taking a moment to touch me as his expression softened, and after laying a piece of gauze on my forehead, he kissed me.

"It's okay, Rai," he whispered, placing my hand back on the gurney as I saw pain flash through his eyes. I knew he blamed himself for my capture, especially since he had been the one to send me to the bathrooms. Kisten touched the gauze gingerly and I wished he would touch my skin, despite the pain it would cause. "You can sleep now."

His words were almost like a spell as I immediately began to pass out. My eyes closed and I drifted off to darkness as the ambulance drove off into the night.

20

I woke up in my own hospital room and wondered where I was for a moment, my side and head still aching. Crispin, Justina, Kisten and LeAlexende all stood in the room, talking in low voices on the other side of the curtain. At the sound of Justina's voice, I sat up, wincing as my body ached from the movement. I clumsily adjusted the hospital gown that I had been changed into and cleared my throat as I prepared to speak.

"Justina?" My voice was hoarse as I called out and the curtain was quickly pulled aside. My friend's eyes welled with tears as she flung herself around me, crying openly and I grunted from the added pain to my body.

"You're alright!" She sobbed and I hugged her back as best as I could. I closed my eyes as I squeezed her, fighting my own tears as the three men joined us. "Raiven, I was so worried about you."

"That's what I should be saying," I retorted softly, pulling back and laying my hand on her stomach. "And the baby?"

"Just fine." She smiled and Crispin came up behind her, wrapping his arms around her midsection before kissing her neck. She shrugged him off and he backed away, still smiling. "Should've chosen a better father, though."

"You wound me." I couldn't help but laugh at Crispin's theatrics and LeAlexende merely shook his head. I turned to face the Overseer as he lifted his phone, excusing himself out of the room. Then I looked at Kisten, who was still standing silently away from me. I leaned away from Justina and reached my hands out to him, wanting to touch him. Justina looked at me, confused and then slowly turned to Kisten, the look on her face becoming accusatory. He stepped toward me and I pulled him closer, pressing my face into his coat. He stiffened under my touch, and I looked up to his face to see his unreadable expression.

"It's not your fault," I whispered, rubbing my face against him as I held him as close as the bed would allow. He relaxed a little at this, and he carefully placed his hands on my gown to return my gesture. I took it as a good sign, and pressed little kisses into his stomach. "I let him take me, I didn't want to risk losing him."

"He hurt you," Kisten said and I looked up at him again, seeing all the pain and anguish he felt over me being hurt. He gently stroked my bandaged ear and I leaned into his hand, the bandages protecting me from the pain. "I should've been there."

"We would have never caught him if you had been and besides, you were there when it mattered," I whispered, smiling up at him. "You saved me from the mess I put myself in, just as I knew you would."

"A feat I'd rather you not repeat." Lucius walked

into the room, followed by Evalyn and LeAlexende. Kisten stepped away from me, and he moved next to Justina and Crispin at my feet as the Overseer walked in. I winced as he stood over me, fully expecting to be punished for my insubordination. "You disobeyed me several times during this case, Raiven. You forget I can tell when you don't listen."

"I didn't forget." I winced, and Eve smiled smugly, clearly enjoying the proceedings. She loved the idea of Lucius punishing me and was practically giddy as she waited to see what he would do. LeAlexende gave her a curious look, but soon looked away, seating himself into the chair behind Lucius. Lucius stood over me for a moment and I slouched into the bed. To my surprise, he placed his hand on my head and I looked up at him, surprised again by his smile.

"And yet, thanks to you, we were able to punish the one who hurt Justina and Irida." He withdrew his hand, releasing me. Eve turned to him, astonished by his words and her disappointment was plain on her face. "I think the injuries you sustained are punishment enough."

"And Irida?" I ventured, my voice soft as I spoke. Lucius smiled again, his eyes gentle. "Is... is she safe?"

"I spoke with Brandon and he gave me leave to release her back to her Overseer and Alpha." I sighed with relief, leaning back into my bed. "Both have also agreed to help her rehabilitate. This experience and the revelation about her partner has left her mind... fragile."

I nodded, closing my eyes as I sank back into the bed. Irida had seemed like a gentle soul and after realizing the crimes he had been using her for, it only made sense that she would have a mental break. Lucius patted the sheets next to me, looking up to my other three companions.

"Since we're all here," he began and I opened my eyes again, wanting to watch the proceedings. "It seems some adjustments need to be made in my Coven."

Justina looked away sheepishly, but Lucius was far from upset. Instead, his eyes were lit up with mirth as he met Crispin's gaze. He glanced toward Justina's midsection, before looking up to her face. "While I am excited for you both, Crispin has seniority here, and considering your age Justina, you will have to relinquish your place as Second."

"That's fine." Justina nodded, and her lover wrapped his arm around her, sneaking a kiss into her hair as Lucius turned his attention to Kisten. Kisten chanced a glance at Eve, before meeting his friend's gaze. Eve looked at him, confused, before turning to look at Lucius' back, her anger starting to grow on her face. She looked like she wanted to say something, but Lucius ignored her as he kept his eyes locked on Kisten's. It was a long time before Lucius sighed and turned to me, smiling as well.

"If you would like, Raiven, you may take her place." Lucius offered and I looked at him, shocked. I was certain that I would've been relieved of the Coven as well, since Kisten was pursuing me as a mate. I turned to Kisten, who smiled, touching my bed sheets near my hand. Lucius continued as I turned back to him incredulously. "Normally, you would take First, since being the Alpha's mate would give you more power over the pack. But I have a reliable First, despite his skirt-chasing ways."

Eve looked as if she would lose her jaw to the floor

and she passed her eyes between Kisten and me. Her surprise slowly turned back to anger, and then to malicious scheming as her eyes rested on me. I knew that she was thinking what I also worried about: being Kisten's mate would cause a conflict of interest with my job and I would have to reveal my true nature as the Immortal. I gave her an equally challenging look, which took her aback for a moment. Eve was also keeping her nature as a Supernatural a secret and if she outed me, I would out her and I was more likely to keep my job, even if I lost my team.

Lucius seemed not to notice the silent fight Eve and I were having with our expressions and continued speaking, laying his hand on my bed again. "You are the next logical choice for Second and a replacement I think Justina would agree with."

"Of course," Justina chimed, leaning forward from Crispin and smiling at Lucius. "Raiven is stronger than me anyway, she could've been Second the moment she came. The only reason she's in this room is because she allowed herself to be."

"Mostly true," I countered, but I said it with a smile as she leaned back, as if resting her case. Lucius turned to me for my answer and I looked down to my feet, flexing my toes under the bedspread. Moving up to Second would pile more responsibility on me, and I worried that it would do more harm than good. Lucius had insisted that I join the Coven thanks to my age and power, but I only agreed to a low spot. It was already dangerous enough that Lucius had agreed to protect me: the closer I was to him, the more likely it was that the Hunters would find him as well.

I felt a hand on my thigh and looked over to

Kisten, who was lightly encouraging me. I sighed heavily, already knowing what my answer had to be.

"I accept, Lucius." I spoke calmly and clearly, the air swirling in the room for a moment before settling back down. Lucius smiled broadly, stepping back as I accepted my new position. "I only hope we both don't regret this."

"If Kisten doesn't, I certainly won't." Lucius answered as he watched Kisten's hand on my leg and he turned to look at LeAlexende, who had watched the proceedings with semi interest. Upon noticing his friend's gaze on him, the Overseer shrugged, looking back down to his phone.

"This is your area, Luc. Your risks are your own." LeAlexende shook his head as he spoke, but both vampires were smiling as Lucius turned to walk away. Eve glared at Kisten and me once Lucius had passed her, clearly not happy with this small victory Kisten had won behind her back. She looked ready to mouth something, but didn't, settling for a malicious grin as she followed her lover out of the room.

Once she left, everyone in the room breathed a sigh of relief and I turned to LeAlexende, who was still sitting in his chair.

"How much longer are you going to stay?" I asked, and the vampire shrugged, not looking up to me.

"Until you're released, I guess." He replied dismissively, motioning toward Justina. "After all, I've spent most of this visit supervising sleeping women in hospital beds. Might as well see it through to the end."

Crispin laughed openly at this, while Justina looked away embarrassed, and I turned to Kisten as he chuckled slightly. LeAlexende smiled brightly, clearly pleased while he engrossed himself with his phone. I returned my gaze to Justina, just in time to see her looking at me. She was looking at Kisten's hand where it still sat on my thigh and she gestured toward it when she spoke.

"So, *cecmpa*[1], when was I going to learn about this?" She inquired and Crispin held her close again, kissing her neck. I looked away, not really sure how to answer her as my cheeks grew warm. I had never shared my feelings toward Kisten with anyone, so her surprise was understandable. Considering how much I complained about Crispin, she probably would've thought I was still stuck on Mikael. At my lack of a response, she turned her attention to Kisten, who was still stroking my leg softly. "Well, Alpha? Since when have you decided to pursue my *птица*[2], hmm?"

"How long have I wanted to, or when did I start?" Kisten asked softly and I turned to look up at him. He was looking at me lovingly and I hummed under his gaze, leaning into him as he pulled me against his coat once more. Justina lightly turned to LeAlexende when he chuckled and then returned her attention to us.

"I can imagine it started once I could no longer interject." She mused, placing her hand on her hips as she sized up Kisten. She then returned her attention to me and I shifted my eyes away again. From the look in her eyes, I knew she wanted to lecture me about keeping Kisten and I a secret. "And this is who you want, Raiven? Whom you've chosen despite everything?"

I nodded my head, looking into her eyes. She must've liked what she saw as she motioned her surrender, moving her hand to her still flat stomach. A small smile started on her face and I felt a soft ache in my chest.

"I guess I'm not one to judge, considering who I chose." Crispin gasped in fake surprise as she jabbed at him, but she didn't turn as she continued speaking. "I know you don't completely approve of him."

"I don't see the appeal," I admitted, and she chuckled at this, reaching up to touch her lover's face. Crispin leaned into her hand happily, nuzzling her palm. I watched their interaction with surprise: I had never seen Crispin act so sincerely towards anyone since my arrival in The Capital. I shrugged, doing my best to smile. "But that's your choice at the end of the day."

"Well, there's some semblance of a good man underneath and all things considered, at least he can still be there once I'm no longer able to." She stroked his chin and the vampire hummed, wrapping both of his arms around her waist. I felt a tinge of pain in my chest at their display of affection, and from Kisten's tightened grip on me, I knew he felt it too. I looked up at him again and he was looking at the couple with an unreadable expression. I pressed a kiss into his coat, and he looked down to me again, a sad look in his eyes. The night we had together was both a blessing and a curse: it had given us a taste of what we could have and it made it harder to be without it.

Kisten released me, mumbling something about finding a nurse for tests as he left the room. He closed the door softly and I looked after him longingly, wishing I had said something before he left. Justina and Crispin soon excused themselves, citing their need to make Justina's next appointment before leaving me alone with LeAlexende. The Overseer was engrossed in his phone, or at least acting like it, so I leaned back into my bed, closing my eyes as I waited for Kisten to return.

21

K isten soon returned with the nurse and they checked my vitals, changed my bandages, and disappeared again. I reached after Kisten as he turned, but he left without so much as a backwards glance and I sank back into my bed, dejected. LeAlexende remained engrossed in his videos, a chuckle escaping him every now and then.

'Sis?' I reached out to her with my thoughts, gently resting my hand on the wood. Since the vampire was ignoring me, I took the chance to speak with her, wanting to check on her after all that had happened. I grew worried at her lack of a response, and I gripped the locket tighter as I reached out again. 'Sis?!'

'Hush... I'm still here,' she reprimanded, and I breathed a heavy sigh of relief as I relaxed my grip. She was struggling to stay awake, and her voice sounded far and distant. 'Good to see... that you're up.'

'Are you alright?' I queried, and she took her time responding, the long silence causing a deep fear to rise in my chest.

'I'll live... for now. Separating me from you was...

reckless... and stupid.' She berated me and I winced under her harsh words. *'I know... you were thinking on your feet... and at least... you didn't run away...'*

'I'm sorry.' I gripped the wood tightly again, my heart beginning to pound as I considered the worst. Without my power to feed on, it only made sense that the locket would have fed on hers. My impromptu plan had cost me valuable time with my sister, time I could never get back.

'You... don't have much longer... to make your choice, sis.' Tears welled up in my eyes at her calling me 'sis', the ache in my heart growing. She was rarely so informal with me, usually using my name rather than a term of endearment. Given our history, it was understandable, but I couldn't help enjoying it when she showed how much she still cared. *'I will... rest as much as possible... and only check on you when... I'm needed. Sound... fair?'*

'Alright,' I conceded, dropping my hand as I closed my eyes to the bright white lights. *'Goodnight.'*

'Goodnight, Raiven.' As my sister faded, I took a deep breath, letting it out shakily as I touched my longer curls. I felt as if my chest would collapse in on itself from the thought of losing my sister; I didn't want to consider the idea of being without her, but I also didn't want her to fade away. If I didn't return her to her body, her essence would simply fade into the ether and it would be as if she never existed. After all we had been through, after all she had done for me, I knew I couldn't allow her to be forgotten, even if I was the only one who remembered.

I was jolted from my thoughts and opened my eyes to see LeAlexende standing, drawing the curtain to hide me from whoever was walking in the door. I froze in the bed, not sure who could have arrived to give LeAlexende such a reaction.

"I do believe you should not be here." The Overseer's tone was calm and he remained standing, his shadow projecting onto the screen that separated us. The other party spoke and my heart froze as soon as I recognized the voice.

"Now I'm not even allowed to visit her?" Aurel insisted, and he was trying to walk past the Overseer but LeAlexende was insistent as well. He blocked Aurel's movements, keeping him away from the bed.

"Even if you were allowed, she is sleeping," The Overseer lied smoothly, and I closed my eyes, trying to steady my heartbeat in case Aurel managed to move aside the curtain. "But I do believe you are not allowed near her regardless, since Lucius told me you were injured recently."

"That was days ago!" Aurel whined and I rolled my eyes behind their lids. Even though he knew the rules, Aurel was willing to use any excuse to be near me, especially with Kisten away from my side. LeAlexende must've sensed the ulterior motive as well, as he dropped his voice as he spoke.

"She is injured, she is likely to lose control if she senses undead blood. The only one allowed in her room is me." The Overseer purposely avoided saying Lucius and Crispin had been here earlier, and Aurel fell right into the trap, scoffing as he tried to push past again.

"If she can stand you, she can stand me." I heard him walk to my curtain and I held my breath as I waited to see what would happen. The door opened again and from the shifting energies in the air, I knew it was Kisten.

"Aurel." He said his name plainly, walking past him. Kisten gently pulled the curtain back, placing the results of my blood work on my screen. He stepped back to the other side, separating me from their eyes once more and I took the chance to open my eyes slightly. "You're not supposed to be here. If you want to talk to Raiven, wait your full five days or–"

"Shut up!" The lich hissed and the power in the air shifted again as Aurel grew angry. Kisten remained calm, placing his tablet down before crossing his arms where he stood. "You have no say in this."

"Considering I'm her doctor right now, I do." Kisten replied coolly, but I could feel his power beginning to rise as he grew angry. "Right now, I couldn't care less about your issue with me. Raiven is still recovering and the only reason Alex is allowed in her room is because Lucius trusts him to be able to restrain her if it comes to that. So, wait out your last day and then come see her if you want to talk to her that badly."

"You can't order me to do anything. You are not my Overseer." Aurel sounded as if he meant to force his way to me, but Kisten refused to move, blocking the lich's access. LeAlexende sat down in his chair loudly, his power beginning to fill the room, overwhelming both Aurel's and Kisten's.

"I don't know what your problem is, Sixth," the Overseer threatened, using Aurel's rank rather than his name to address him. I heard the two men turn to the vampire and from what I could see of their shadows, LeAlexende was looking at his phone again. "But you will not threaten the safety of my charge. I am responsible for Raiven as long as she remains here.

"So, you can leave," the vampire paused, and I could feel his annoyance in the air, a slight wind blowing through the room despite the window next to me being closed. "And wait until the end of your five days or I will escort you out, and I will make sure Luc knows how willing you are to break his rules."

Aurel seemed to take LeAlexende's threat to heart, as I soon heard him walk out the room, slamming the door behind him. The air returned to normal as LeAlexende relaxed and Kisten sighed heavily, running his hand through his hair.

"Competition?" LeAlexende asked quietly, and Kisten scoffed, dropping his hand. He appeared to glance at the shut door, considering his answer.

"More like an obsession. You know how Aurel can be when he wants something." Kisten sighed again, his voice soft as he spoke. "And how poorly he takes being denied."

"Hmmm, more like he still hasn't gotten over you." The Overseer offered and Kisten remained silent. I saw his hand on the curtain again and closed my eyes as he pulled it back to look at me. I steadied my breathing to mimic sleep, and he moved the curtain back to separate us.

"That too, but to be honest, I haven't gotten over it, either." He admitted, sitting down in the chair across from LeAlexende. He slouched in the chair, clearly worn out from his labor. Even though I was his main concern, Kisten was on shift today, and was only checking on me in between his other patients. He let out a heavy sigh, almost groaning as he continued speaking. "He is *not* going to let me court her without a fight."

"Well, does your courtship have anything to do with him?"

"No," Kisten answered, and then he sat up, holding his hands in front of his lap. The pair remained silent for a moment and then Kisten spoke softly. "I love Raiven. I want her because of that, not to get back at him for what he did. But... I'll admit, I always intended to flaunt it in his face, and that was before I knew he wanted her."

Kisten sighed, leaning back in his chair, slouching as his feet slid across the floor. "I enjoy showing him that I have what he wants. That he was wrong about me, and I beat him. He thought she would be his so easily and I just..."

Kisten made a grabbing motion with his hands, cupping them as if he were holding a delicate flower; his voice was soft and loving and my chest ached with his words, "... snatched her away. And now she's going to be mine."

"So?" The Overseer offered, putting his phone down as he looked up to meet Kisten's gaze. I desperately wished I could see my lover's face, but I remained silent, maintaining my façade as they spoke. "Are you going to stop pursuing her again? Are you going to let Aurel have his way?"

"No. Never." Kisten's response was immediate, and I smiled at his words, my heart pounding. The Alpha sat up again, his posture determined. "I... stopped myself once from pursuing her because I thought it would be better for both of us. I was wrong. If I won't allow my own worries to stop me, I won't allow him to get in my way."

"Good to see you still have some fighting spirit. A part of me worried you had lost it." LeAlexende chuckled, slouching in his seat and looking back to his phone. Kisten chuckled as well, standing from his seat.

"Never, Alex. I'm still here to save you when you need it."

The Overseer laughed as Kisten went out and we were left in silence again. I almost sat up, wanting to ask the Overseer about Kisten's words, but decided against it, lying back on the bed.

"How long are you going to stay quiet?" LeAlexende's voice startled me, and I jumped slightly as he pulled back the curtain, smiling at me knowingly. I shrugged, closing my eyes.

"Well, I figured I shouldn't let Aurel find out you were lying," I retorted and LeAlexende chuckled, leaning against the wall. I chanced a glance at the Overseer, my eyes drifting to the closed door to my room. "And... it didn't feel like I should interrupt your conversation with Kisten."

"Well, do you have anything to add, Raiven?" The Overseer's gaze betrayed his bright smile and I frowned, returning my eyes to the ceiling.

"I don't like being in the middle." I admitted, closing my eyes as I sighed. "I know they have their issues and I'm not saying Kisten's wrong, but I don't like him using me to get back at Aurel. But... Aurel is really the one making it a huge problem, all because he wanted me for his harem."

I sighed, looking over to LeAlexende again. The Overseer hadn't moved and was still watching me with the same expression and my frown deepened. "I should've told him long before now about my feelings for Kisten, but honestly, at this point I don't think it would've made a difference."

225

"Want an outsider's opinion?" The vampire offered and I nodded, waiting for him to speak. LeAlexende moved next to the bed and took my hand. He squeezed it slightly, stroking my skin before speaking. "Aurel would've made it about him and Kisten even if Kisten had chosen someone else. He may say he accepts Kisten's decision, but he never will, no more than he'll ever accept yours. Would you like to know exactly what Aurel told Kisten when Kisten turned him down?"

I nodded again and the vampire squeezed my hand again, releasing me as he leaned against the bed, facing away from me. His voice was soft when he resumed speaking.

"Kisten left The Capital that night and came to me in the Southern Grove." I couldn't help the shocked look on my face and LeAlexende chuckled, sensing my surprise despite not seeing my face. "I was shocked, too, until he told me what happened. Aurel had told him that Lucius kept him bound via the Oath because no one else would ever risk being with someone like him. That he was a bound animal, only to be used by its master and had no other value than that use."

I was stunned into silence. I had never imagined Aurel could say something like that: he could be harsh with his words when he was upset, but not only had he tried to demean Kisten, he went as far as to accuse Lucius of being like Mater Vitae. My hands curled into fists at my anger and LeAlexende glanced back at me, his expression amused.

"Of course, when I brought Kisten back, I told Lucius what I had been told." The vampire turned away from me again, his voice holding back his obvious anger at the memory. "Aurel was dropped from third to sixth then, but Lucius wouldn't get rid of him thanks to his power. I warned him then that Aurel would only become more of an issue as time went on."

"I'm guessing Lucius said he'll deal with it?" I offered and LeAlexende laughed, turning to face me again.

"You have gotten a good grip on him in your short time here." The Overseer chuckled and I couldn't help but smile back. LeAlexende took my hand again, his eyes boring deep into mine as he spoke. "I'll tell you the same thing I told him: be wary of Aurel. He only does whatever he thinks will get him his way, and I have no doubt there is no limit to how far he'll go."

"I will, Alex. Thank you." With this, he released me and returned to his seat, resuming his video surfing on his phone. I sank against the pillows, reflecting on what LeAlexende had told me.

What would Aurel have said to me to get me to choose him? I wondered silently, and then I gripped the sheets tightly. *What will he say?*

I shook my head to try to free myself of these thoughts. I rolled on my side, wincing from the pain as I closed my eyes, hoping to sleep away my turmoil.

22

I sat on my couch in the warm afternoon, flipping through channels as Lira and Xris lounged around me. The pet sitter was surprised to see me home without notice, but I was happy to finally be allowed to rest. Brandon had visited me while I was in the hospital and insisted that I stay home for a few days. The team was getting ready to fly out on a new case, but he was adamant that they would call me if I was needed.

I accepted his demand easily: I didn't really want to get back to work so soon. It wasn't the first time I had ever been injured on a case, and I never felt like jumping back in afterwards. I almost convinced myself to tell Brandon the truth but stopped myself. I knew I would have to speak with the Director first, and it would ultimately be his decision as to what happened next.

Kisten released me the day after Brandon's visit and took me home, my car having already been driven from The Dream for me. My two cats were excited to see me after the additional week I had been gone and I was equally happy to see them, crouching down immediately to pet them. Kisten had left silently after seeing me inside, not giving me the chance to say goodbye as he closed my front door behind him.

I hadn't heard a word from him in the past day, and a pit began to form in my stomach as I checked my phone for the millionth time. I wasn't surprised he hadn't come by, but I had expected at least a phone call or a message. My thoughts turned to Eve's mischievous smile at the hospital and Aurel's insistent visit shortly after, causing me to groan loudly into the pillow.

"He won't give up," I tried to reason with myself, lying down as I settled on my usual cartoons. I almost expected my sister to respond, but she remained withdrawn. She hadn't spoken to me since the hospital and if it wasn't for her occasional presence to see how I was doing, I would've thought she had already faded completely. As she had pointed out, eventually I would have to make my decision: to allow her soul to fade into obscurity, or to give her peace by returning it to her body.

The pit in my stomach increased with these thoughts and I groaned out loud, causing my cats to stand up and shift their positions, clearly not wanting to deal with my anguish. I tried my best to pay attention to the colorful characters on my screen, but my own thoughts kept me from paying much attention to the lighthearted cartoon.

A sudden knock at the front door made my heart race and I nearly ran to the door, about to throw it open, when I forced myself to pause. Taking a deep breath, I glanced out the peephole, wanting to make sure it was Kisten before I threw myself into the arms of a stranger. I had nearly done it earlier with another delivery man, who was merely dropping off my monthly order of food for my cats. He was clearly taken aback as I flung the door open and I was more than embarrassed as I signed for the box.

It was Aurel, the lich leaning on my porch railing as he waited. My heart sank again, but not only from disappointment. Aurel's insistence that I choose him over Kisten was truly making me despise him and I regretted agreeing to be friends more and more. After LeAlexende's warning at the hospital, I knew that I had to treat Aurel as a serious threat, and my heart began to pound. He knocked on the door again and I merely leaned against it, wishing for him to go away. I noticed his shadow against my curtained window, and I knew he was trying to see if I was in my living room.

I'm sleeping, go away. I don't want to see you. I thought as he knocked a third time, his patience decreasing with his pounding. I considered locking myself up in my room in case he tried to force my door open, but I forced myself to remain still, lest he heard me walk away. I wanted to look out the peephole again but was too afraid I'd see him trying to look in for me.

"I know you're there, Raiven!" He finally growled and I stiffened, too worried to breathe. I felt my sister's presence rise, but she remained silent as we both waited to see what the lich would do. He pounded on the door again and I had to cover my mouth to hide the sound that tried to escape me. "I just want to talk!"

'I'd hate to see what he'd do... if he wanted to do more than talk.' My sister sneered and I nodded silently, jumping again as he continued pounding on my door. I slowly began to back away as I saw my door frame move with his pounding. The last thing I wanted was to face Aurel if things got physical, but I knew I would have no choice if he forced my door open.

"Raiven, please." His voice was soft now and I could hear him leaning against the door. I scoffed: now he wanted to plead with me, as if he had not just been pounding against my door like an angry ex? "I just... I just want to talk to you without him around."

After a moment of silence, I heard him place something on the doorstep and walk away. He paused for a moment at the end of the porch, presumably turning back to look at my door, but he soon continued walking and I breathed a sigh of relief as his car started in my driveway. I waited until I could no longer hear his motor as he drove off down the street before I opened the door, seeing a small package on my doormat. There was no note attached and I looked at it cautiously as I picked it up and closed my front door.

I held the package with disgust, angry that Aurel would even consider leaving me a gift after all that he had done. Knowing him, it was probably a piece from his jewelry collection, trying to show me that he really cared about me, but I didn't want it. It was nothing more than a trap and I was determined to throw it away as I walked back into my home. I was in no way prepared for the solid mass I ran into as I stepped into my kitchen, a blast of cold air also greeting me.

"Distracted?" I nearly flung the package from my hands as I threw my arms around Kisten. My side door was open, and my cats pawed at the screen door, wanting the freedom of outside as I embraced my love. Kisten pulled me closer to him, planting soft kisses into my hair. "It almost seems like you missed me."

"Of course I did." I breathed, resting my chin against his chest as I looked up at him. Kisten smiled down at me, and I leaned up for a kiss, him meeting me halfway. I almost moaned at the searing pain of our lips slanting across each other, but I had missed kissing him more than anything. Kisten pulled back before I could deepen the kiss and stepped away, turning around to close my side door. I placed Aurel's package on the counter as I walked up behind him, unable to keep my hands off my Alpha.

"How did you get here?"

"I ran." He said and I turned him around, trying to measure if he was joking. He still had the same smile on his face as he stroked my scarred face down to my injured earlobe. I had insisted he remove the bandage before releasing me and I was shocked by how normal it still looked. The bullet had taken off a decent amount but it was still less than I expected, something Kisten said amounted to the bullet also grazing my face as I had moved, therefore slowing it down ever so slightly. I leaned into his painful touch, pressing his hand against my face and I closed my eyes as he continued. "I was talking with Lucius."

"About?" I asked, my eyes still closed as I took in him being here with me. Kisten chuckled and I lazily opened my eyes to see his grin.

"Us." Kisten stated, pulling me into another embrace. He kissed my ear, and I sighed happily despite the burning pain. "There are more steps to courtship, and I was going through them with Lucius, including when I would be released from the Oath."

"Hmm," I hummed in agreement, burying my head into his chest. His shirt smelled heavily of sweat even though the fabric was dry, so I knew he must have run from the Landing in animal form. He pressed more kisses into my hair, before looking away from me and his grip on me suddenly tightened. I followed his gaze to the package on my counter, still wrapped and unopened.

"Who's that from?" He asked, and I froze, not wanting to tell him Aurel had been here. He looked at me darkly as my heart pounded and I kept my gaze away from him. His voice was dark and full of suspicion as he spoke again, this time speaking directly against my skin. "Raiven, who is that from?"

"It's fro—" I barely got a word out before Kisten pinned me to my counter, pushing his body into mine. I gasped at the sudden movement, wrapping my arms around Kisten's neck as he lifted me on the marble and began to assault my neck, burning my skin with his licking and biting. I moaned openly at his assault, and he wrapped one of his arms around me, sliding my groin into his as he leaned over me, undoing the buttons of my shirt with his free hand. He growled into my skin, and I moaned for him, loving every second of this punishment.

"Don't accept gifts from him," He commanded, sliding his hand up my stomach once the fabric fell open. I clung to him uselessly, only able to nod at his command. He licked up my collarbone, a trail of pain following his sandpaper tongue. "I don't care if they pile up on your doorstep. I don't want you to touch them. Let me take care of them."

"If you punish me like this, why would I listen?" I moaned and Kisten paused in his torture, pulling back slightly to look at my face. My eyes fluttered open as I breathed heavily, my body full of pain and my desire for him. His eyes were swirling, and he growled above me, the sound causing my midsection to clench with promised pleasure and pain. "I won't touch them, Kisten."

"Good." With no small ceremony, Kisten lifted me off the counter and over his shoulder, jolting me from my stupor. I heard him scrape the package into the trash before carrying me out of the kitchen, and I knew his intentions before we reached my bedroom. He tossed me on the bed, climbing on top of me before I could even finish bouncing from the impact. His mouth was already back on my neck, and I wrapped my legs around his waist, pulling him closer to me. As I surrendered to the painful pleasure of his touch, I knew I had chosen correctly.

LeAlexende lounged on the train station bench, placing his phone down next to him. It seemed the Overseer had exhausted everything he could do, and he slouched, running his hand through his blond hair. He pulled a few strands in front of his face, grunting before pushing them back with the rest. His expression was pensive as he glanced up towards the dark night sky, breathing heavily.

"Sorry I'm late." LeAlexende looked down to see Lucius walking towards him alone, finally without Evalyn tailing behind him. He sat next to him on the bench, and for a moment, the two friends took in the empty station, devoid of life. The silence was deafening: no wind to blow around the debris and trash, no insects to sing their nightly song. A perfect setting for two undead beings to speak and LeAlexende gently placed his hand on top of Lucius'. The Overseer immediately weaved their fingers together, closing his eyes.

"Sorry that your visit was disrupted like this. It

was... not ideal." Lucius was first to break the silence, slouching to match LeAlexende. He sighed heavily, and LeAlexende snorted, closing his eyes as well.

"This is your territory: I didn't expect a peaceful visit. Even without Raiven's case, you keep too many dangerous people around," LeAlexende straightened himself and sat up properly on the bench as he released Lucius' hand. A train flew by in the quiet night, interrupting the silence with its noise. LeAlexende watched it with semi-interest as it passed, the lights a blur as it flew by. It left as quickly as it came, bringing with it the façade of life as the wind of its passing moved his hair in its wake. LeAlexende lifted his hand to his hair again as he spoke. "It's more than enough that I got to see you."

"What did you come for? You don't usually visit without warning," Lucius asked, chancing a glance at his friend. LeAlexende didn't answer at first, keeping his gaze on the darkness the train had ventured into. "I know the holiday worked as an excuse, but it's not like you to take a risk like this."

"Basina... is dead." LeAlexende closed his eyes, a painful expression on his face. Lucius' eyes widened in surprise, and he stammered to answer.

"But...she—"

"He finally got her. I heard it from her Retainer." LeAlexende continued, ignoring Lucius' surprise. His expression was heavy and it was clear the news was difficult for him as well. "With her gone, we're the last high ranking First left."

"Just less than half of the original Thirteen now." Lucius sighed, and LeAlexende nodded, his blond hair rippling as his fingers passed through. In a moment, his hair turned white as fresh snow and his purple eyes had deepened almost to black. Lucius was unsurprised by this change and merely looked on as LeAlexende stood. His face and form also seemed different somehow, but his voice sounded the same when he spoke.

"Lucius, I'm the only one left who truly remembers and with Basina gone, I'm the last of the Siblings. It's only a matter of time now before he finds out I'm here." LeAlexende's voice was barely above a whisper and Lucius looked as if he was about to argue. He was stopped, however, as LeAlexende raised his hand in front of Lucius. "There needs to be someone else who remembers."

"Alex, please, don't do this. It'll weaken you too much. If he is after you, you need all of your strength." Lucius pleaded, even as he knelt underneath LeAlexende's hand. It was obvious he didn't want to, but it was almost as if he was being forced to comply. "Let me go get a memory device, that should suffice—"

"No, Luc. We need to do this the old way and you're the only person I trust." LeAlexende insisted, and Lucius was crestfallen at his friend's words. "You need to feel my memories. You need to know the Truth."

Lucius nodded through silent tears, and LeAlexende smiled a sad smile as he brought his wrist to his mouth. He pierced his own skin with his fangs and allowed his blood to drip over Lucius' face. His purple eyes began to glow, and the white hair swirled in the wind his power had called forth.

"Enkidu." LeAlexende used Lucius' human name,

causing Lucius' power to come forth on its own. Lightning flashed in the sky above the pair, a storm beginning to form over the train station. "Accept the blood of Mortem and allow my memories to be yours."

With this, Lucius opened his mouth, allowing the blood of his friend and fellow Overseer to flow into him. The storm above them grew in turmoil and LeAlexende lifted his eyes up from Lucius. His eyes seemed to meet mine as the lightning flashed and I woke up as the thunder crashed above the pair.

It was dark in my room after the flash, and I could hear Kisten sleeping peacefully next to me. I carefully stood and walked to my window, seeing the brewing storm on the horizon. I could feel my sister's presence and without words, I knew she was thinking the same as me.

"What was that?" I wondered aloud, and a thought flashed through my mind, my sister pushing the concept to me. "Necromancy..."

Despite my own necromancy saving me from being turned into a vampire, it was not an ability I really ever used. I had only used it once in my long life and that was when my sister died, to bind her soul to the locket. Mater Vitae had forbidden me from ever using it and even after I left her, I had never felt the need.

Necromancers were extremely rare among humans, to the point that most never knew they were one unless they accidentally called upon the power. Just as sorcerers were considered dangerous, necromancers were considered a worse threat, given their ability to raise zombies.

"That's impossible, sis. Necromancy doesn't work on the undead." I rebutted and she left, not arguing with me. I continued looking at the still-growing storm, still trying to process what had happened and what I had seen. Another First was dead: that was the real reason LeAlexende had come to visit. If what he said was true, more than half of the First were now gone and that meant the Hunters would soon be closing in on the few who remained. I gripped myself tightly, my room briefly filling with light as the lightning flashed again.

'Don't...' I was surprised by my sister's voice, and I gripped the locket as she came back, her frustration obvious. I glanced to the floor, afraid to see my own reflection in the glass. *'Don't you run this time. Don't you give this... up out of fear.'*

"I..." I started to dispute her assumption but I stopped myself. I always ran when I knew the Hunters were getting close and I felt the familiar urge to flee now. I turned to look at Kisten, who was still sleeping peacefully on my bed. My heart pounded as I looked at him and I gazed back to the storm that was growing ever closer. LeAlexende had been worried enough that he had wanted to share his memories and power with Lucius and my Overseer was known for his habit of taking risks. Staying with him meant putting everyone in The Capital in more danger but... leaving him meant losing Kisten. Losing everything.

I sighed deeply, pulling myself away from the window and back to the bed. Kisten rolled over to me, draping his arm across my waist as I sat down. I couldn't help my smile as I laid back down, gingerly touching his face with my fingertips. Kisten sighed happily in his sleep, leaning into my touch as my fingers ached with pain. I gripped my sister's locket as I closed my eyes, my heart and mind filled with determination.

'*Don't worry,*' I assured her, breathing deeply as she faded away. '*I won't.*'

ABOUT THE AUTHOR

Kirro Burrows grew up on the sandy beaches of Florida, so they know a thing or two about having their head in the clouds. Creating new worlds and exploring character dynamics is the air they breathe and crafting thrilling, realistic stories are their bread and butter. When not traveling for inspiration, Kirro can be found decorating beautiful cakes in their kitchen while caring for their blooming family or sneaking some work on their illustrations and comics. There's always something new going on with them, and that's the way they like it.

To learn more about Kirro Burrows and discover more Next Chapter authors, visit our website at www.nextchapter.pub.

NOTES

CHAPTER 1

1. Latin "Thank You"

CHAPTER 2

1. Russian "Geez" or "Oh my"

CHAPTER 3

1. Irish "my Love"

CHAPTER 8

1. German "The pup"

CHAPTER 10

1. Russian "Sister"

CHAPTER 16

1. German "Bird"

CHAPTER 18

1. German "my love"

CHAPTER 20

1. Russian "Sister"
2. Russian "Raven"

Catch A Raven
ISBN: 978-4-82415-780-5
Mass Market

Published by
Next Chapter
2-5-6 SANNO
SANNO BRIDGE
143-0023 Ota-Ku, Tokyo
+818035793528

25th November 2022